A FINE LINE

By Emma Leigh Reed

This book is a work of fiction. Names, characters, events, places and incidents are either the product of the author's imagination or are used in a fictitious manner. Any resemblance to actual persons, alive or dead, events or locales is strictly coincidental.

Text copyright © 2015 by Emma Leigh Reed
Cover art design by Gemini Judson

All rights reserved. Published by Tiny House Publishing, LLC in the United States.

No part of this book may be reproduced or transmitted in any form by any means, electronic or mechanical, including photocopying, recording, or by any information storage and retrieval system, without permission in writing from the author.

Visit us online at www.tinyhousepublishing.com

ISBN (paperback) 978-1-944550-07-3
ISBN (eBook) 978-0-9967270-9-9

The text of this book is set in 12-point Times New Roman font.

Formatting done by Colleen McCready
Edited by Sara Cremeno

Printed in the United States of America

First Edition

To Todd

An amazing friend, who helped make this book what it is today. Thank you so much with the inspiration of Xander's poem.

Chapter One

Grace McAllister glanced around the crowded room. She knew she looked the perfect grieving daughter dressed in a conservative black dress and black pumps. Her long brown hair was pulled back into a sleek bun. She was grieving, but this wasn't the way she wanted to be doing it. Her mother, Abigail McAllister, had been very popular in this small town. She had run many committees and her hand had been involved in all that had gone on, from making sure the downtrodden had food on their pantry shelves to helping people perfect their resumes in looking for a job.

Abigail had been the epitome of what a small town should be—people helping others and taking care of their own. Although Grace had agreed with everything Abigail had stood for, she couldn't help but shake her head that there was more to life than this. She wanted more.

Grace sat straight backed, hands folded in her lap, her eyes downcast as the minister droned on and on about her mother's attributes. Grace felt grateful for the life she had known growing up. They hadn't lacked anything, and Grace had opportunities that most kids just didn't get unless they were of the wealthy class. She cringed. She hated that people still associated her with wealth. She had wanted to do more and had insisted that

Abigail not give her anything else but allow her to live on her own. Grace had completed her degree in elementary education and loved her job as a second grade teacher. She made a decent living and loved her one bedroom apartment, which paled in comparison to her childhood home.

The last song started and Grace stood with the rest of the congregation paying their respects. She pasted on her smile saved for these occasions and greeted the townspeople coming through saying condolences. She nodded and smiled. Her cheeks ached and Grace wished more than anything she could head home and slip into a hot bath. Her feet were killing her. She wanted to kick off the dreaded shoes and go barefoot. Abigail would understand; she knew Grace's preference for bare feet that had followed her through childhood into her adult life

She hesitated a brief moment as a man standing a few people back made eye contact with her. He wore a leather jacket and jeans. His dark chocolate eyes pulled her attention to him. She cleared her throat and glanced back at her mom's elderly neighbor, trying to focus on what she was saying.

"Thank you, Mrs. Smythe, for coming. I know you will miss Mom."

Grace smiled and nodded through one more person before the handsome man in leather stood before her. His grip on her hand warmed her to the core, heat flooded her face.

"I'm sorry for your loss." His deep voice, kept low just for her ears, flamed the fire starting within her.

"How did you know my mother?" Grace tried to slide her hand out of his, but he kept his grip.

"I, personally, haven't seen her in years. But I'm here out of respect for my parents, who knew her." He smiled and squeezed her hand before letting go.

"Wait." Grace reached out, laying her hand on his arm. "Who are your parents?"

He patted her hand. "I'm not sure you would know them." Before she could respond, he had moved out towards the door. Grace inwardly groaned in frustration. She didn't know who he was or who his parents were.

She continued, nodding, making the appropriate comments as the line moved on. She sat down as everyone left the church and headed next door to the fellowship hall for some food. The town's Women's Auxiliary had prepared a feast in honor of Abigail, who would have normally been the one in charge of these types of deals. Grace sighed. She just wanted to go home and put this all behind her.

"Are you hanging in there, Gracie?"

Grace glanced up and saw Reverend Sawyer. "Yes, sir. Thank you. You did a beautiful job today. Mom would have been so pleased."

"Everyone loved her and will miss her greatly." Reverend Sawyer held out his hand to her. "Don't you think you should go next door and mingle with those who are here for you?"

"Of course." Grace stood and smoothed her wrinkleless dress into place. "Thank you again."

Grace screamed internally. She still was made to feel two years old, being told what to do. My God, she was a grown woman of twenty-five! Couldn't she decide if she wanted to mingle with people or just go home? She could hear her Mom now. *Gracie, shoulders back. Never let people see you're upset. Be strong and do the right thing.* She was so tired of doing the right thing.

Entering the fellowship hall, she found fewer people had stayed than she feared. Finding a clear path to the coffee, she made her way there. It was slow progress, as people stopped her, sharing stories of her mother. Finally, reaching the coffee, she reached for a cup. Her hand stilled when she heard the voices. "She'll be just fine. She's a good girl. Never was in a bit of trouble."

Grace poured her coffee and held it as she closed her eyes. Always the good girl. God, she hated that phrase.

"Going to sleep?" The familiar deep voice brought her eyes open wide as she turned towards him.

"No. But it would be nice if I knew who you were."

"My apologies. I guess I forgot to introduce myself. Xander."

"Xander...?" Grace waited.

"Just Xander."

Keeping her face neutral, Grace glanced up and down, taking in his appearance. "I'm glad you came. Although it might have been a bit more appropriate to dress in something other than a leather jacket and jeans." Grace bit her bottom lip. Her mother would have killed her for sounding like such a snob.

Xander's deep laughter brought a smile to her lips. "It probably would have and I apologize for my appearance. See, I just got into town this morning, just moments before the service started. It was either go change and be late for the service, or show up on time like this. I felt this was the lesser of the two inappropriate behaviors."

"A man who is on time. That is definitely a positive attribute to have."

Xander placed his hand under her elbow and led her to a quiet corner. "I have a feeling you would rather be somewhere else."

Grace looked around the room. This was her hometown, her family in every sense. These people had watched her grow up, had supported her through tough teenage times—like when her dad died—or shared her victories, like when she graduated high school and college. How could she resent being here? She turned towards Xander. "What makes you say that?"

Xander sipped his coffee, keeping eye contact. "A hunch. I think the 'good girl' may not want to play that part right now."

"Play a part? What are you talking about?" Grace pondered his words. He was right. She wanted to do something spontaneous and forget who she really was—whoever that may be.

"I can see it in your eyes, beautiful eyes by the way. You want to shrink away from these people and be anywhere but here. Can't say I blame you. Funerals give me the creeps. I would prefer to pay my respects to someone I love in a way that they know would be unique for only me."

"Kind of hard to do that when you're held to a higher expectation by everyone around you."

Xander nodded. "Screw expectations. They always fall short, anyway."

She tried to stop it, but the giggling bubbled up inside of her and escaped. Grace covered her mouth with her hand. Gaining control, she glanced at Xander. Amusement radiated across his face, his eyes twinkling.

"Now that's a beautiful sound, Grace."

She shook her head. "It's inappropriate to be laughing like that at my mother's funeral."

"Why? Did Abigail never hear you laugh?" He scowled. "I bet she loved hearing that sound from you, and would love it on a day like today, of all days. You laughing, remembering your mom for the woman you knew her as, not the one that everyone else saw."

Grace smiled. "Mom *was* a different person at home. You know, she used to dance around the kitchen and sing. Of course, she couldn't carry a tune if her life depended on it, but how she loved to sing." Grace stared into her coffee cup, snared by the image of her mom dancing with her dad in front of her. Grace had loved seeing the love shine from both of them. It was like she wasn't even there when they were in each other's arms. Her mom had always told her *Never pass up a chance to dance with the man of your dreams, Gracie. It's like heaven on earth.*

"See? Remember her for what she was to you, Grace. Not to everyone else." Xander took her empty cup. She stood there watching him walk to the trash can to throw them out. His jeans fit snugly and the muscles rippled beneath them. She wished he had removed his jacket so she could see the rest of him.

"You ready to get out of here?"

"I can't go, Xander. I need to stay while people are here." She shook her head slowly.

"Wait right here." Xander wandered off. Grace watched him corner Mrs. Smythe and speak to her. She nodded her head and waved goodbye to Grace.

"Let's go. You have permission from Mrs. Smythe."

"What did you say to her?" Grace quizzed him.

"Just that you were tired and I was going to make sure you got home." Xander again placed his hand gently under her elbow and led her from the room. Once outside, Grace stopped and took in a deep breath.

"Thank you. I don't know how you did it, but thank you."

"I did nothing. You want a ride home?"

Grace glanced around and the only unknown vehicle in the parking lot was a motorcycle. "On that?"

"Yeah." Xander smiled. "I have an extra helmet."

"Ummm, no. I'll walk. It was nice to meet you though, Xander." Grace hesitated. "Who are your parents again?"

"I don't believe I said." Xander smiled and turned towards the motorcycle. "You sure you don't want a ride?"

"No, thank you."

"You've never ridden one before, have you?"

Grace felt her face flush. "No."

Xander stepped close to her. "I won't let anything happen to you. Let your hair down and hold on to me if you're scared."

Grace met his eyes. "I'm not scared."

"I'm thinking you are, but you probably aren't 'dressed appropriately' anyway."

Grace's eyes widened. Xander's mouth twitched as he tried to hold in the laughter. Her laughter mixed with his as she punched him in the shoulder. "Go, wise guy."

She turned towards home and started walking away, thoughts running through her mind of Xander and his motorcycle. She would love to ride with him, her arms wrapped around his waist, head against his back. She sighed. It would never happen. Nice girls didn't ride motorcycles. She made a mental note to ask Mrs. Smythe if she knew his family. Xander was a mystery, one she hoped was just passing through town. She couldn't afford to be sidetracked from all she had to do now that Mom was gone.

Ever the perfectionist, Abigail had made Grace a list of exactly what needed to be done. First, she had a meeting with the lawyer, and then of course, Mom had insisted that Grace move back into her childhood home. Grace shuddered at the thought. She loved her one bedroom apartment and had no desire to move back into the mansion that lay on 72 acres of sprawling farm land. Her mom had always wanted horses, but before making that decision, the cancer diagnosis had come through and everything changed. Mom's focus suddenly became on fighting the cancer and putting her affairs in order. One of the things she had made Grace promise her was that she would fill the barns with horses. Grace had no desire to have horses and wondered how much Abigail would haunt her if she reneged on that promise.

Grace let herself into her apartment, leaning against the closed door. The darkness filled the room. At that moment, Grace couldn't find any positive elements in today or what the next few months, let alone years, might hold for her.

Chapter Two

Xander rode his motorcycle through the quiet town. Today he had done the unimaginable and showed up at Abigail McAllister's funeral. His parents would be horrified when they found out. He was headed there now. He slowed the bike as he turned into the winding driveway that ran a mile into the property before the Stevens' house appeared.

For as long as he could remember, Gracie McAllister had been the socialite of this small town. Abigail had given her the best of everything. He had secretly wished Abigail had been his mother growing up. He knew how she treated everyone in town, and she was always very kind to him when their paths crossed, even when she knew who he was. As a teenager and in his wild days, he had been in quite a bit of trouble. Abigail had met with him quietly one day, instructing him to get his life together and she would do what she could to help him on that front—as long as he never told his parents.

Xander had known only pieces of the feud that had gone on forever between the Stevens family and the McAllisters. He had seriously been crushing on Grace in school and seeing her today only brought back a flood of emotions. She still was just as beautiful as he remembered and he had to remember to breath when he was close to her. He only knew that he was never supposed to talk to Grace in school and his father went as far as sending him away to prep school to ensure they stayed apart. Xander had kept tabs on Abigail and Grace over the years. He hadn't made it back from college in time for Mr. McAllister's funeral, but had sent Abigail a letter with his condolences and his gratitude for the kindness she had always shown him. She had sent him cards every now and then, remembering special occasions for him – graduation from prep school, college, and even his birthday every year.

Xander never knew why Abigail took such an interest in him, but he was grateful for her actions. His own mother could never remember his birthday and felt it was a sign of weakness to acknowledge things like graduation except with some sort of status symbol. He had received new cars for each one of his graduations. Cars that he had sold and never driven. He preferred the motorcycle. The feel of the road beneath him, the curves allowing his body to be one with the bike.

Xander parked his motorcycle and hesitated at the bottom of the front stairs. The house was cold, never exuded warmth, even when he was young. He dreaded this reunion. He was twenty-seven years old and still felt like a child when he came home. He sighed and climbed the five stairs to the front door. He rang the doorbell and wondered if Grace had to ring Abigail's door bell to visit. No, he could guarantee that Abigail would have gone around back and slipped right into the kitchen, probably finding Abigail there making cookies or something.

The door swung up and Gerard, his father's butler, stood there. "Greetings, Sebastian, sir."

"Hi, Gerry."

Gerard stepped back a step and gestured him inside. "Please, sir, don't call me Gerry."

Xander smirked. "Please, sir, don't call me Sebastian. You know I prefer Xander."

Gerard nodded. "Your father is in the study."

Xander smiled and shook his head It would always be the same. "Thanks, Gerard."

"Sir." Xander didn't know how he did it, but Gerard disappeared without a sound, leaving Xander in the foyer of the house. God, he hated this house and all its grandiosity. It was all for show. This house was no more a home than a beehive for a puppy. . He wandered down the hall to the study and knocked quietly on the door. He almost prayed his father wouldn't answer.

"Enter."

Xander pushed open the door and walked in.

"Sebastian, I didn't know you were coming home." His father rose and waited for Xander to come into the room and sit down.

Xander slid into a chair and gestured for his father to sit. "It was a last minute decision. I heard about Abigail McAllister's death and wanted to pay my respects."

"Why? She was nothing to this family."

Xander sighed. "She was a kind woman who lived in the same town you did for years. It was the right thing to do."

"Sebastian, I don't need to tell you that our family has nothing to do with the McAllisters. They were beneath us and we really don't need to attend those types of functions."

Xander stood, his fists clenched at his sides. John Stevens could be a cold man, but even the words coming from his mouth were nothing short of icicles. "You never change." Disgust exuded from his words and Xander turned towards the door.

"Sebastian Alexander, sit down!" The command stopped Xander in his tracks. Even as an adult, he couldn't deliberately disobey his father. He turned and slid back into the chair. Stared at his father.

John pushed back in his chair, tapping his fingers together. "What is it you are really doing here?"

Xander shook his head. "I told you. I came to pay respect to Grace regarding his mother's death."

"You have always been told to stay away from that girl."

"And you sent me away to ensure it, didn't you?"

"I sent you away to the best prep school there was so you could have a proper education. Nothing more than that."

"Yeah, right." Xander stood. "I really would like to say hello to Mother."

John gestured, dismissing him. "She's probably out in the garden."

Xander wandered into the kitchen as he headed to the back gardens. Stopping just inside the kitchen door, he closed his eyes. The smell of fresh baked bread and yeast assaulted his senses. He could pick out the distinct aroma of garlic coming from the oven. The smells awakened his senses bringing him back to a time in his life where the kitchen was the middle of his comfort zone.

"Now, Xander, my boy, you better come right over here and give me a hug." Hattie's voice brought back memories of his favorite place in this house. The round woman gestured him closer. Her ample size ready to be engulfed into a bear hug.

He pulled Hattie into a hug. Hattie, the cook, had always been his favorite. She had mothered him when he was sick, given him a place to hide when he couldn't stand the coldness of the house and gave him more support than he could ever remember anyone else giving, although Abigail McAllister had been a close second.

"Whatcha doing home, child?" Hattie waved her hand for him to sit on a stool while she went back to mixing whatever sweet she had started.

"I went to Abigail McAllister's funeral today."

"Good for you, honey. That woman loved you."

Xander's face lit up. "How do you know that, Hattie?"

"Child, I would spend my day off over at Ms. Abigail's home. She was so good to me. I kept her updated on what you were doing. She was always so concerned that your father tried to keep you from her Gracie."

"Why? Why couldn't I be friends with Grace?"

Hattie shook her head. "I don't know the whole story. All I know is..." The back door opened and in stepped Elizabeth Stevens. She was the picture of perfection as she glided into the room.

"Sebastian." She pulled him into a quick hug before smoothing her perfect dress and her hair. She gave an unconscious shake to rid herself of the repulsed contact.

"Mother." Xander had a soft spot for his mother, even if she was not the warm, affectionate mother he had always wanted, but that's where Hattie had come in. He supposed he was fortunate to have a mother and a cook who acted like his mother.

"How long are you staying?" Elizabeth laid six long-stemmed roses on the counter, which Hattie immediately picked up to fuss with. "Those are for the foyer, Hattie."

"Yes, ma'am."

"I'll probably leave tonight, mother. Father doesn't seem all that thrilled that I am here."

"Nonsense. You know your father. You are welcome anytime. Please stay at least until tomorrow. We haven't talked in so long."

"I can stay the night, but just so you know, I came for Abigail McAllister's funeral."

Elizabeth's face immediately turned stone cold. "You didn't tell your father that?"

Xander stared at her. "Of course I did."

"Why, Sebastian? Why do you have to agitate him so?"

"I went because it is the right thing to do, not to cause you or Father any discomfort."

Elizabeth smiled too brightly. "Dear, it's okay. I know you have a heart that sometimes is too kind to the undeserving. You just haven't learned when to keep those things quiet yet."

"I have nothing to keep quiet, Mother. What are you afraid of?"

Elizabeth shook her head. "What time is dinner served, Hattie?"

"Six, like usual, ma'am." Hattie busied herself with arranging the flowers.

"Fine. I will see you then, Sebastian. And no talk of this funeral at dinner." Elizabeth fled the room.

Hattie patted him on the shoulder. "Child, some things never change."

"I still want to talk to you, Hattie, about this stupid feud."

Hattie waved her hand. "You need to go now. I have to finish dinner. We'll talk later."

Xander sighed as he wandered out into the back yard. He sat down at the patio table and took in the scenery. The acres behind the house sprawled out before him. He couldn't remember a time when the lawns weren't perfectly manicured and the hedges immaculately shaped. His own reality right here was that this was the perfect home and he was the rebel child who was sent away to avoid causing a blemish in this family.

At the end of the property, although not quite visible from the house, stood an old cottage that Hattie had occupied since she was brought on as a cook. Xander had spent many evenings down there watching TV with her, eating popcorn. Hattie had encouraged him to be free with his thoughts and to make decisions based on his wants and needs, not those of his father's. Xander had thanked her by never mentioning to his parents where he came up with the idea he could express his thoughts. In some aspects, being sent away from home was the best thing that had happened to Xander.

He had been able to pursue his own dreams. His father insisted he get a law degree. Xander had changed his major to marketing, graduating top of his class. His father threatened to cut him off for that change, but for once Elizabeth had stood up to her husband and begged John to be lenient with their son. Xander had spent the last four years doing freelance marketing work, allowing him to move from place to place, never settling. He kept his bad boy image, and in fact, thrived on it.

His father would be horrified to know about the tattoo on Xander's shoulder, a lion that reminded him of the strength he had come to find in himself. He glanced at his watch. Five o'clock. He had an hour until dinner. Not time enough to go check on Grace. How he wanted to see her again. He had been itching to pull that hair out of that blasted bun since the funeral. When he had told her to let her hair down, he had definitely meant literally, along with figuratively.

Xander moved from the table to a lounge chair next to the pool. He slipped off his leather jacket and lay back. His sunglasses in place, he closed his eyes and felt the tension leave his body. The sun warmed him, and he felt tempted to take off his T-shirt. He smiled. Grace would have been shocked if he had taken off his jacket at the funeral and showed the tight fitting shirt. He wondered how she felt about tattoos. Had she ever wanted to cut loose and rebel against the expectations set so high for her?

Expectations. He hated that word. It suffocated him.

Chapter Three

Grace slipped into her yoga pants and a tank top. Pouring herself a glass of wine, she wandered out to her balcony. The lights remained off in her apartment. The sun had just started to go down over the horizon. She looked up and lifted her glass in silent salute to her mom. The Abigail she had known and loved hadn't been the same one she took care of the past couple of years.

Abigail had become a shell of a person Grace had known as the cancer ate away at her. She continued to love music, but the dancing had ceased. Grace had watched her mother slip away little by little. If the truth was told, Grace had been grieving her mother's loss for the two years prior to her actual death. Xander had been right. She needed to remember her for who she had been, not the person Abigail portrayed to others. The real Abigail– the one that hurt more deeply, yet never showed her tears; the woman who put everyone ahead of herself, but would be in need and never tell a soul. Grace had learned all the lessons she had been taught about never letting anyone see your vulnerabilities.

So Grace sat in the shadow of her balcony, drinking wine, tears coursing down her face as she remembered her mom. The physical pain ran deep and she cried at all she had lost, and for the unknown future, unsure of what she should be doing now. Her mother had been her rock, her encourager and biggest fan. No matter what Grace did, her mother showered her with love. Grace knew that not everyone had a childhood like that.

She thought about all the townspeople that had showed up for the funeral. One dominating family stood out as being absent. She had heard stories of the Stevens family right here in town. Although she never met them, they were known for hating everyone and for some reason, hating her mother most of all. Grace never knew the reason and Abigail never talked about it. Abigail simply said some people get consumed by hate and can't find their way to be good people.

After the first glass of wine was gone, Grace brought the bottle out to the balcony with her. What was the point of having to get up to keep filling it? Tonight she was indulgent and tomorrow she would put on her "good girl" persona and do the right thing for all to see.

Her doorbell rang just as the sky had become dark. Grace startled at the sudden intrusion into her quietness. She contemplated not answering. Hadn't the townspeople had their fill of her today? As the doorbell rang a second time, Grace cursed silently and made her way to the door.

With a deep breath, she slowly opened the door.

"Hey. Figured you hadn't eaten so I brought dinner."

Grace blinked her eyes. Three glasses of wine and she suddenly started hallucinating. Xander stood at her door! She gripped the handle tighter, hoping for a brief moment he would go away before stepping back allowing him access.

Xander stepped inside and handed her a covered dish. "It's still warm, so go grab a fork and start eating."

"What?" Grace, realizing this wasn't a dream, glanced from the dish in her hand to Xander.

"Did I wake you?"

"No. I was sitting on the balcony." Grace pointed and then glanced down at the plate in her hand again. The aroma teased her and her stomach rumbled in response. "Oh, my. I guess I am hungry."

Xander chuckled. "Come on. Go back out on the balcony and I'll get you a fork."

Grace allowed herself to be pushed towards the balcony as Xander headed towards her kitchen. She sat down at the small bistro sized table, her wine glass and bottle still there.

"Here." Xander set the fork down in front of her.

She dug in with gusto, the mashed potato and pot roast with carrots and onions hitting the spot. This was comfort food. "Why?" She asked between bites.

"Why what? Bring you food?" Xander watched her, amused as she nodded. "I just figured you might be hungry, and I wanted to see you again."

Grace paused. She laid her fork down and sat back. "You wanted to see me again?"

Xander met her stare. "Of course. Love your hair down, by the way."

Grace self-consciously grabbed the ends of her hair and attempted to twist it back into a bun.

"Please, leave it down. It suits you."

She felt herself blush as she continued to eat. "So tell me about yourself."

Xander shrugged. "Nothing to tell, really."

"Who are you? How did you know my mom?"

Xander paused. "I met her years ago as a child. She was kind to me and I never forgot it. I've lived away for years now."

"You grew up here?" Grace pushed the plate away and refilled her wine glass. "Do you want some? I'm sorry, I don't have anything else."

"No, I'm good." Xander shook his head slowly. "I did grow up here."

"Why don't I remember you? We must have gone to school together."

"No, I want to private schools." Xander cleared his throat. "So what's next on the agenda for you?"

"You don't like talking about yourself, huh?" Grace sipped her wine. "Okay, but we're going to finish this conversation at some point. I'm a teacher, second grade. I love those kids so much.

It makes me feel like I'm doing something worthwhile."

Grace talked nonstop for the next couple of hours about her work and her mother's influence on her wanting to be a teacher. She suddenly stopped and glanced into the darkness realizing how freely she had chatted after so much wine. "I've talked your ear off. You probably have someplace to be."

"I've enjoyed it. I probably should leave you now, but would love to see you again before I head out of town."

Grace stood. "I don't know."

Xander ran his finger around a ringlet framing her face. "Let me take you for that motorcycle ride."

Grace stood still. Heat coursed through her. She wanted to, wanted to so much. "I don't know."

"You said that before. Come on, Grace, let me show you how much fun letting your hair down can be." Xander leaned towards her. "You don't always need to be the good girl. Cut loose."

His lips were close to hers and Grace wanted to taste them. She wanted to run her tongue along his. She closed her eyes. She had never felt this way before about anyone.

"Say yes, Grace."

She opened her eyes. The lump in her throat stopped any words from coming out so she simply nodded.

Xander smiled and stepped back, his fingers leaving her hair. She suddenly felt cooler and longed for that heat again. "Tomorrow morning. I'll pick you up at ten. We'll get out of town and go for lunch up the coast."

She nodded again as she followed him to the door. He turned towards her and brushed a kiss against her cheek. "Wear jeans, sneakers and bring a light jacket."

He was gone before she could respond. Grace leaned against the door. She had just agreed to go on a motorcycle. She waited for the panic to hit her, but instead felt nothing but excitement. Guilt hit her briefly. She should be grieving not swooning over a man, yet she couldn't help but be thankful she felt beyond grief and pain.

Chapter Four

Xander woke with the sun shining. It had been years since he had felt so excited and nervous about being with a girl for a day. He typically kept his dating very casual, never wanting to give a girl the wrong impression. But Grace was different. He wanted more with her. For the first time ever, he could envision a life that involved a family. Where did those thoughts come from? He was here only a short time and then headed back to his carefree lifestyle, going place to place and working as he felt he needed to.

He slipped into the kitchen, eating a quiet breakfast, wanting to avoid running into his parents today. A chill always crept over him when they were around. He would check into a hotel in town today. He wanted to stick around to get to know Grace better, but he couldn't stay here.

"Boy, why are you hiding in here? Your parents are wondering if you are coming to breakfast." Hattie startled him as she came up behind him.

"I can't have breakfast with them this morning. I'm headed out for the day."

Hattie gave a small laugh. "What are you up to?"

Xander paused for a moment. "I'm spending the day with Grace McAllister."

"Ohhh, boy, you better be careful." Hattie smiled. "She's a sweetheart; don't you be pulling your love-her-and-leave stuff on her."

Xander's hand went to his heart. "Me? I'm not like that."

Hattie smacked his hand down. "I'm serious. You be good to her."

Xander kissed her on the cheek. "Yes, ma'am."

"You better go before your momma comes through here. Get going."

Xander grinned as he waved good bye and snuck out the back door. It almost felt like his teenage days when he constantly snuck out to cause trouble. He had only landed in jail once, but had caused enough heartache—more likely disappointment—in his parents that he had been shipped out, hidden from this town and any gossip that he might bring upon the family.

Pain sliced through him at the loss he realized he suffered through as a teenager. There had been no supportive parents, no warm home life. He had grown up in a cold, stifling household that had pushed him into acting out for attention. He hadn't done anything really bad, but enough that he had been labeled the bad boy. A label he found he enjoyed.

He arrived at Grace's at exactly ten a.m. She must have been watching for him because she stepped out before he got off his bike. She stood nervously on the front steps as he approached her.

"Morning."

"Hi." Xander held out his hand to her and waited until she placed her small hand in his.

"You ready for this?"

Grace nodded, but then shook her head no. "I'm not sure."

"Piece of cake." Xander helped her put on the extra helmet. He straddled the bike, and then placed her hand on his shoulder. She soon got situated behind him. She tentatively rested her hands on his waist.

"Ready?" He called back to her as he started the motorcycle.

"Yes." Her hands fisted his jacket. He grabbed her hands and slid them around his waist, squeezing her hands. He eased the bike onto the road and stayed at a slow pace until she started to relax.

He kicked it into a higher speed, occasionally reaching to touch her hands reassuringly. He loved the feel of her arms around him, her thighs fitting snuggly around his hips. He grinned. Yes, they would be a perfect fit if they got more intimate. He turned towards the coast and relaxed into Grace's arms. This he could get used to.

Grace loosened her arms just a bit, but didn't want to let go of Xander. She watched the scenery go by and realized how at ease she felt on the motorcycle. She leaned with Xander, allowing her body to be one with his on every turn. Instinctively she trusted him. And the reassuring touches he gave her hands, and occasionally rubbing her leg, played a huge part of that trust. He cared that she had been nervous. He had started slow and increased speed only after she had relaxed a bit.

Grace's thoughts were filled with the need to do more. She was tired of being the good girl. She reflected back to the telephone conversation that morning with the lawyer. He wanted to have her come in Monday for reading of the will. She was an only child. She figured everything had been left to her—that was before the lawyer said he was pushing it to Monday because he was still trying to locate the other heir. Fear had clenched at her chest, tightening her airway at the thought of someone unknown being close enough to her mother to be an heir. The news of another heir had almost led her to break her date with Xander.

Date? Was this really a date?

They rode for an hour before Xander pulled over at a rocky drop off. The view of the ocean amazed her. Grace shook her hair out after taking off the helmet. Turning to Xander, she simply grinned. "Wow."

"Right? It's spectacular." Xander grabbed her hand, leading her to the guardrails. "There is nothing better than this to take away the stress and worries of the day."

"Just what I needed this morning." Grace squeezed his hand.

"Everything okay?"

Grace nodded. "Just some unexpected news this morning. Nothing I can't handle." She almost laughed at her words. She had no clue how to handle another heir to her mother's estate. Who could this heir be?

"There's a great restaurant about thirty minutes from here. Great seafood, if that's okay with you?"

Grace turned back towards the bike. "Sounds perfect."

They continued on and Grace felt perfectly at ease on the motorcycle. Xander was well aware of his surroundings and an excellent driver. She could have leaned against the back rest and not held onto Xander, but instead she kept her arms around him loosely, enjoying every touch between them.

Grace had always hated silence. She constantly had music playing whenever she wasn't busy, or even just as background noise. She had inherited that from her mother. Abigail had loved music, all genres of music. Grace had grown up listening to big band music, jazz, classical and rock. Yet, on this ride with Xander, she enjoyed the silence. The rhythm of the bike, the humming as it ran over the road, brought a sense of peace to Grace that she had never experienced in her twenty-five years of life. She understood how Xander thought this was the best way to travel.

They pulled into a semi-empty parking lot outside a beat up building. As Xander shut off the bike, he grabbed her hands before she could get off. Holding them with one hand, he released the strap of his helmet and slid it off. She freed one hand, but Xander refused to let go of her other one. She mimicked his steps of releasing the strap and removing the helmet.

"What is this place?" She whispered close his ear.

"Only the best seafood you will ever taste." Xander leaned back against her. "Are you ready for a new culinary experience?"

Grace caught her breath. She wanted to just hold on tightly to this moment and never move from Xander's side. She nodded as he watched her, entwining his fingers in hers. She smiled and leaned into the contact. Heat scorched her, and she feared she would never recover from the flames that were igniting between them. She sensed he felt the same, as his eyes flickered with uncertainty. Had he never had an experience like this, either? She couldn't imagine it. He was the bad boy type, one that probably had women falling all over him.

Grace felt his fingers slide from hers and he sat up, allowing her space to get off the bike. A rush of cool air brought the heat between them down a notch. She slid off the bike and stood looking at the building. In what she considered true Xander style, he placed his hand under her elbow and led her to the door. He had gentleman qualities. Surely he had grown up in a household that valued chivalry? Grace once again found herself wondering about his past and how she never knew him if he grew up in the same town.

They entered the building. Grace strained to see beyond them into the dining room. Lighting was poor, but the building was homey.

"Sit anywhere." A voice called out from the bar against the far wall. Grace turned, not noticing it at first.

"Come on, over by the windows. Trust me, the food is much better than this place looks." Xander escorted her to the table and held her chair for her as she sat down. The view outside the window overlooked the ocean. Waves gently lapped the rocks along the edge of the water. Heaven. Grace couldn't think of another word that could describe this day so far.

"How have I never known about this place?" Grace questioned after they placed their orders and rolls had been placed in front of them.

"It's advertised mainly by word of mouth, although I have been trying to get Rocky, the owner, to do a bit more marketing."

"Your specialty?" Graced watched Xander as he seemed to pick his words carefully.

"One of my specialties, I guess. I have a marketing degree and do some freelance work from time to time."

"What other specialties do you have?"

Xander grinned. "Taking good girls out of their comfort zone."

Grace sat back, a thoughtful smile played across her mouth. "And what do you know about my comfort zone?"

Xander waited until the waitress had set down their plates. Grace's shrimp and his scallops were still steaming, and the freshness beckoned him to dive in. He popped a scallop into his mouth and chewed carefully. "I know that conservative look you wore yesterday was a comfort zone for you. Your hair pulled back in a bun, making you look older than you are. Do you have any idea how beautiful you are with your hair down?"

Heat crept up Grace's face as she shook her head. Xander reached for her hand. "Don't be embarrassed, Grace. You're beautiful and sexy. I have a feeling you haven't been told that near enough in your life."

Grace started eating the shrimp, making it impossible to answer. She glowed inside at the words he said even as her mind balked at them. He was right. No one had ever told her she was beautiful, except her mom, and well, that just didn't count. Sexy? Well, that was not a word she would ever associate with herself.

"Anyway...what else do you do for full time work?" Grace finally spoke.

"That is my full time work, the marketing, I mean. I do the freelancing because I don't like to be tied down in one place. I like my freedom to move around and meet new people, just experience life." He sipped his beer. "I don't have a lot of bills by continuing to move. It keeps my life simple, easy."

Grace nodded. "How do you stand it though? Don't you have family you miss?"

Xander sat back and watched her. "I can honestly say I don't."

"You don't have family?" Grace was shocked.

"That I miss." Xander stared out at the ocean. "Not everyone has a mom like Abigail."

Grace reached her hand over and covered Xander's. "I'm sorry. Everyone should have family they can count on to love them and support them."

Xander flipped his hand, putting his palm to her palm. Their fingers melted into each other's. "Thank you, Grace." He felt her sympathy through her touch, saw it in her eyes and it cut him to the core. He hadn't thought in a very long time, before this return visit to home, how much he had missed out on. His childhood was one of the reasons he had vowed never to have kids, or even marry. His parents were superb role models for a bad marriage and terrible parenting. He couldn't fathom being as loved as Grace had been growing up. She had no idea what she did to him—not only bringing out the emotions, but physically, he wanted nothing more than to pull her into his arms and let her know that he was okay.

At least, he was now that he had found her.

Grace had pushed her empty plate aside and watched Xander as he finished his beer. "Are you going to tell me who you are? You said your parents knew Abigail."

"Grace, let's not do this. You don't remember me and let's just start with getting to know each other as people who just met."

"Wait. You said I don't remember you. I *did* know you, then."

Xander nodded slowly. "Our paths crossed a time or two in middle school. I left in high school for a private school."

"Please, Xander, tell me who you are." A look of frustration passed through her eyes. It tore him apart to cause her that frustration, but he was more afraid of her anger when she found out who he was.

"Grace, can this wait at least until we get back? Please?" He hated the vulnerability he felt when looking at her. He wanted her more than anything, and the thought she would shun him could bring him to his knees. Big bad Xander brought down by her. His best friend, David, would never believe it, or let him forget it if it happened.

Grace simply nodded. She didn't want to push him. The pain in his eyes made her want to just hold him close and let him know it was okay. She had no preconceived ideas about childhood school mates she didn't even remember. She wracked her brain for who she would have known that had moved away. She came up blank. They started their journey back home, Grace lost in thought hoping he was thinking of her as much as she was him.

Chapter Five

Grace unlocked her door as the phone started ringing. "Come on in." She called to Xander behind her as she dashed for the phone. Xander closed the door quietly as he came in

"Hello. Yes, of course I remember you." Grace stood listening, watching Xander. "Yes, of course. I will be happy to meet with you next week. You remember Abigail's house. Yes, I understand I will need to move back in there. Thank you so much for returning my call. I look forward to your help." Grace hung up the phone and leaned against the wall. Xander had not moved from the door, looking like he was ready to bolt at any moment.

"Do you want to come in and sit?" Grace pointed to the living room. She prayed he would stay, but knew he wanted to avoid any conversation around them knowing each other.

"Grace." Xander crossed the hallway, stopping in front of her. His hands landed on each side of her waist, pulled her close to him. She raised her hands and laid them on his pectorals. His muscles twitched under her touch and she closed her eyes, willing herself to not throw herself at him.

"Grace." His voice was a whisper, flowing over her, pulling her closer. His lips touched hers softly, gently caressing her. She leaned into him, parting her lips, her tongue stroking his. He groaned softly and broke off the kiss. "Grace, I should go."

Grace stepped back. A wave of cold ran through her. He was running away. She drove him away. Her mind froze as she realized he watched her.

A soft sighed broke the silence. "Don't. Please don't. I'm not going anywhere."

"I didn't..."

"You were thinking it. Grace, I want to get to know you better. I'll be sticking around for a while, until you tell me to go."

"You don't have to go now." Grace's voice trembled. What was she asking of him? Did she even know how far she could go with this?

"I need to. Grace, I need to get to know you and right now, I just want you...physically." Xander kissed her quickly on the lips and turned towards the door. He glanced back briefly. "I'll stop by tomorrow."

She nodded and watched the door close behind him. It seemed like hours that she just stood there. Finally, shaking her mind clear she pulled herself together and took in her surroundings. Well, her mom's friend, Hattie, was going to help her locate someone to help her clean out the house. She knew she needed to start packing up things in her apartment. She hated giving this place up.

Thankfully, being a teacher at the beginning of the summer meant she was free 24/7 to get things done. She only had a meeting Monday with the lawyer. *Oh mom, what have you done? Who did you include in this will?*

Her childhood home had been on the outskirts of town. Her parents' property had abutted Mrs. Smythe's property and on the other side had been the Stevens'. She never had met the Stevens family, only heard about them. They had heard they had two sons, yet Grace didn't remember either one. One had been quite a bit older than her and the other only a couple of years. Funny, she hadn't thought of them in years.

It had always been a taboo subject. With a sigh, Grace decided it was time to visit Mrs. Smythe and see if she knew who Xander was. She pulled her hair back into a long ponytail and headed to her car. It was too far to walk to her mom's house, although she could use the exercise to work out some of this frustration building up in her.

She arrived at her childhood home. She just couldn't bring herself to call it her home. This was a place she had left, moved on from. Why did she feel like she regressed? She opened the door and stepped into the foyer. The roses she had placed there a week ago, before her mom had gone to hospice, were dead in the vase. She grabbed it and headed to the kitchen. Rage overtook her as she tossed the flowers into the trash. She threw the vase into the sink, it shattering into a million pieces. How could her mom leave her like this? Cancer. That dreaded C-word that seemed to wreak destruction at every turn.

Grace leaned against the counter, tears falling from her eyes. A faucet inside her had opened and she felt powerless to stop the flow of tears. They poured out of her, a reminder of how strong she had been the past two years, doing the right thing, taking care of her mom even when it was nearly impossible for her to do so. She had hired someone during the day while she taught, but spent evenings and nights here. Her sleep had been next to nil and yet she pushed on and taught during the day, some days feeling like her eyes were full of sand and that she could hardly move one foot in front of the other.

Grace took a deep breath and quieted the flow of grief. She needed to move on. Abigail would not have wanted her to cry over her. She turned on the radio and the sounds of Louis Armstrong filled the room. She choked back the tears that threatened once again. Her mother's favorite. Would it ever get easier? She thought she had done her grieving. Her relationship with her mom had not been the same since the chemo had pretty much cancelled out her mom's ability to function in daily life. Two years had been a long time and Abigail had wanted to go. The last six months before her death, Abigail had slept nonstop and barely conversed with Grace. When they did talk, Abigail pushed her to do things after her death, made Grace promise to do things that she didn't want to do.

Grace shut off the radio with a snap. Irritation surged in her and she knew realistically it was all part of the grieving process, but how she didn't want her perfect day with Xander to be marred by being here at this house. Why had she come? The thought of Xander and Mrs. Smythe talking at the funeral, giving her permission to leave, came to mind. She needed to speak with her.

Determination pushing her forward, Grace headed to Mrs. Smythe's home. She knew once she got her talking, Grace would have a hard time leaving. She prayed that it would be a story she wanted to hear. Fear slowed her steps at the front porch just a bit. What if she really didn't want to know who Xander was? Why couldn't she just let him be the man that brought her happiness? Allowed her to do what she wanted and had no expectations of her?

Grace turned and walked back to her car. She didn't want to know. She wanted to be free and

Xander could be just that ticket to freedom for her. A spring in her step at her decision brought a smile to her face. She flipped on the radio in her car and for the first time in a long time, sang along much like her mother used to, out of tune.

Once home, Grace changed into yoga pants and a tank top. Grabbing a glass of wine, she moved to the balcony with a pad of paper and pen. Her life was about to be changed on Monday, once the reading of the will was done. She knew deep down that her mother had planned something that Grace didn't want to do or be any part of. She took a deep breath and decided it was time she made her own bucket list and do things she had always wanted to do but never had the courage.

Her mind wandered to the past few years prior to her mom being sick. Her mother had always said she supported her, but it was support of whatever kept the right public view of Grace. She was not to run wild, not to do anything outrageous to draw attention to herself. Abigail had constantly reminded her of troubles that other kids go into and how it would mar their life even when they finally got their act together. *Once done, it couldn't be undone.* Her mother's favorite saying.

Grace sighed. She wanted to travel, see places she had never been. She cringed at the thought of doing those things by herself. She wanted to have fun with someone, not by herself. All her life she had been a loner. One that hadn't been invited too much during high school because everyone knew her mother's view on things and felt it was easier to not have Grace involved in parties or their times out getting into minor trouble. There was no minor trouble in Abigail's mind, it was always black and white. No gray areas—ever.

She rode a motorcycle today. One thing she had always wanted to do. She had yet to start her bucket list and was already crossing things off. Her mind drifted to Xander. She was at ease around him. In her gut she knew Abigail would roll over in her grave at Grace spending time with him. She would have considered him a bad boy. He dressed the part, not caring less what others thought of him. Grace envied that.

Grace doodled on the paper. There was no list started, just wistful thoughts that she couldn't bring herself to put to paper. A bucket list wasn't the same as realistic dreams. Dreams were obtainable and opened up your life to improvement. Grace stood suddenly and went to the kitchen. She threw the paper on the counter and sighed, rinsing out the wine glass. Maybe TV would take her mind of Xander and all that she really wanted. Did she want Xander? Or just the image of what she could do if she let her hair down?

Chapter Six

Grace awoke to the raining pounding on the roof. Turning towards her window, she took in the grayness of the day. She guessed today was the perfect time to start packing up some of her stuff. Her mood matched the color of the day.

She had no sooner showered and gotten dressed when she heard the doorbell ring. Opening the door, she found Xander, water dripping from his dark brown hair. He held out a box from *Daisy's Bakery*.

"Breakfast?"

"My favorite indulgence." Grace reached for the box and gestured for him to enter.

"Maybe a towel would help me not drip all over your carpets."

"Of course." Grace returned in a jiff, towel in her hand. "Here, but don't worry about the carpets. They will be cleaned as soon as I'm done packing."

Xander followed her into the kitchen. He leaned against the doorframe as Grace busied herself making coffee. "You're moving?"

"Well, yeah. I'm going to have to move back into my mom's house."

"Why?"

Grace turned to face him. "Because it's what she wanted."

Xander shook his head. "Do you always do what you're told?"

"No, yesterday I got on a motorcycle." Grace smirked.

"Very funny." Xander dropped the towel on the back of chair and stepped close to Grace.

"I have to do what is expected of me." Grace whispered.

"There's that word again, expected, expectations...you are never going to please everyone. When do you do what makes Grace happy?"

"Who says I'm not happy?" Grace shot back, crossing her arms in front of her.

Xander reached up and pulled the elastic from her hair, freeing her hair from the ponytail. "I think when you pull your hair back, you are in your *pleasing everyone else* mode and not yourself."

Grace reached for the elastic. His fingers closed around her hand and held it to his chest. "Tell me I'm wrong."

"It's not that easy."

Xander grinned. "Who said doing what makes you happy is the easy thing? People get pissed at you when you stop putting everyone first."

"You sound like you know that from experience." Grace wanted to pull her hand away, but she felt his heartbeat and it pulled her to lean closer to him. Her face warmed as her free hand went to his bicep. She looked up and met his eyes. Heat shot out of them and he groaned softly, wrapping his arm around her waist and pulling her against him. His lips caressed hers, the gentleness pulling at her. Her tongue danced with his. The beep of the coffee maker signaling it was ready broke them apart. Xander leaned his forehead against hers.

"Coffee's ready."

Grace nodded. "How do you take it?"

"Black."

Grace poured two mugs and doctored hers with sugar and cream. She handed the mugs to Xander and turned to pull a couple of plates from the cupboard. She opened the box and inhaled the scent of the fresh baked glazed donuts. "My favorite."

Xander sipped his coffee and watched Grace bite into the donut. Glaze coated her lips and her tongue ran along them, licking up every drop. Xander shifted as his jeans became uncomfortable while he watched her. Her eyes half closed and he could envision her face as he brought her to orgasm. He shook his head. He felt like a hormone crazed teenager. This wasn't just some girl that would roll into bed with him. He didn't want her to. He wanted her more than just physically – he wanted to know what made her enjoy a donut like it was better than sex, wanted to know her deep-seeded fears and suppressed desires that she felt she couldn't let go of and achieve because of what everyone else thought.

Grace pushed the box towards him. "Don't make me enjoy these by myself."

Xander smiled. "But it's heaven watching you. Do you realize how you let go and just enjoy it? What else do you enjoy like that?"

"Not much, really. I love teaching, but even that has taken its toll over the past couple of years. In taking care of Mom, and teaching during the day, I'm exhausted. This summer vacation will be good to rejuvenate me before I welcome my new second grade class in September."

"Second graders, like seven year olds?" Xander cringed.

Grace laughed out loud. "You don't like kids?"

"I didn't say that."

"You're facial expression did. How can you not love them at that age?"

Xander shook his head. "I like kids, but a roomful of seven year olds seems overwhelming to me. They aren't exactly quiet at that age."

Grace reached for another donut. "You really shouldn't have brought these. These are my kryptonite."

Xander pulled the box out of her reach. "Then show some willpower. I selfishly bought them for myself."

Grace stood and snagged another donut. "Don't even think of trying to keep these from me." She grinned at him. "So what are you doing here this early, anyway?"

"Well, my plan was to steal away today and do something, but the weather has changed my plans a bit. The motorcycle isn't the most comfortable in the rain."

"What if I already had plans?"

"Did you? Besides packing, which I can already tell you are not thrilled about?"

Grace finished her coffee. "Well, not exactly, but I could have."

Xander grabbed her hand. "So what would you have done if you had made plans?"

Grace played with the mug, refusing to look up. "I don't know. I don't live a very exciting life."

"What do you want to do, but never had the guts to do?"

Grace glanced up. She sat back and closed her eyes, pondering the question. "I don't know. There is a lot of stuff I would love to do, but it's just not…appropriate."

"Oh, do tell. What inappropriate thing does the good girl Grace want to do?"

Grace cringed. "Good girl? Really?"

"Yup, there is that same horrified look you had at the funeral when you overhead people talking about what a good girl you were. Come on. Talk to me. Horrify me." He grinned at her.

"Well, I want to travel."

"That's not something that would shock people. You can do better than that."

Grace stood and rinsed her mug. She leaned against the sink, facing Xander. He was serious. Could she reveal her deepest secret wishes? "Maybe cut all my hair short and dye it red."

Xander shook his head. "That's not shocking, except it would be a shame if you cut that beautiful mane you have."

Grace sighed. "See, I don't have any shocking things I want to do." She moved to the living room and straightened pillows on the couch.

Xander followed her and watched her nervously flutter about the room. He knew she wanted more. He could tell by the way she enjoyed her day yesterday on the motorcycle, something she felt was not the *good girl* thing to do. He reached for her hand and pulled her down to sit on the couch beside him.

"Talk to me, Grace." He entwined his fingers with her. "Share with me what you want to do."

She tightened her grip on his hand. "I always wanted a tattoo." Her voice was so low Xander thought he imagined it until she glanced up at him.

"What kind of tattoo?"

Grace's face glowed as a blush spread. "A small rose on my shoulder."

Xander grinned. "Then do it."

Grace's eyes widened. "Are you crazy?"

"Why not? No one will see it unless you want them to. We are the only two that ever have to know you did it."

A tingling ran through Grace. Excitement? Could she actually do it? "Do you have a tattoo?"

Xander nodded. He lifted his short sleeve to show off his shoulder. The lion was high on his bicep. Grace ran her fingers over it. She raised her questioning eyes to his. "It's to remind me that I'm stronger than I used to think I was."

"You needed to be reminded you are strong?"

"Of course. We all have our insecurities, Grace."

"Let's do it." Grace stood and pulled at Xander's hand.

"It's still raining."

"They don't do tattoos outside, right? Do you know where to go? Come on, we'll take my car." Grace's voice rambled on as she left the room to go grab her sneakers.

"Are you sure? It's permanent. Be sure it's what you want to do." Xander reasoned, but in his mind he applauded her choice.

Grace returned to the living room, sneakers on and jacket in hand. She threw her car keys at Xander. "Let's go."

"Grace?"

She smiled. "Yes, I want to do this. You're going to be beside me, right?"

Xander grinned. "Absolutely. There's a great tattoo parlor that my friend owns a couple of towns over."

Xander glanced over occasionally as they drove as Grace sat silently. Xander didn't answer, just simply nodded as the quiet words she spoke, "Mom would roll over in her grave."

Xander glanced over at Grace. She was relaxed, much like yesterday. His mind drifted to the moment he had decided to get his tattoo. He had made the decision out of rebellion, rebellion of the rigid life he had been told he would live. His parents didn't know about it, but it had been liberating. It was like it gave him permission to do what he wanted, and yes, it gave him the courage and the strength to live his life as he wanted. He wanted Grace to find that same courage. To break from the mold she felt she had to conform to.

"Are you ready for this?" Xander broke through Grace's thoughts.

"Yeah, I believe so."

"Don't do it if you have any doubts." Xander gave a weak warning. He wanted her to do this.

"Really? You are the bad boy trying to get me to break away from the good girl image and now you're telling me not to do it?"

"Bad boy? I'm not a bad boy."

"Oh, you are. A bad boy is a simply someone that would make a parent cringe if you brought them home." Grace was so matter of fact that Xander choked back his laughter.

"Abigail would have cringed if you brought me home?"

"Well, from appearances she would have. You showed up to her funeral in a leather jacket and jeans."

Xander feigned shock. "Right, and I do believe you put me in my place as being inappropriate."

"I'm sorry. I never should have said that to you."

Xander waved off the apology. They continued on in silence until Xander parked next to the strip mall. "We're here."

Grace looked around. Her stomach fluttered as butterflies took over. Xander squeezed her hand. "Ready?"

She nodded. As they entered the tattoo parlor, Grace appreciated how tastefully decorated it was. Artwork hung around a small waiting room filled with comfy chairs and a couch. A spiced candle burned in the corner.

"Xander, my man." A deep voice came from across the room.

"Dave. It's been a long time."

The two men shook hands. "You ought to return phone calls once in a while and it wouldn't be so long."

Xander grinned. "You know me, never in one spot long enough to return a phone call."

"Looking for a new tatt?"

"Not me, my friend, Grace, here."

Dave turned towards Grace and took her in head to toe. "What are you looking for?"

Grace turned towards Xander and at his smile, she took a deep breath. "A rose, small, on my shoulder."

"You sure?" Dave's skepticism came through.

Xander stepped closer to Grace. "You're the best, Dave. That's why we're here."

Dave nodded. "True. I'm the best." He pulled out a book and flipped through pages until he came to various different pictures of roses. "Choose what you want and we'll get started."

Grace glanced at the different pictures. There were so many. She finally decided on a small open rose, no stem. Xander concurred it was the best choice for a first tattoo. She giggled. "You think I'll get another one after this."

"I think once you get one, you'll love it and definitely will want another."

"But you only have one."

Xander shrugged. "Doesn't mean I haven't wanted another. Just haven't decided on what I really want."

Grace slipped the strap of her tank top down and off her arm, baring her shoulder. She trembled slightly as Dave washed the area. Xander pulled a chair over in front of her and grabbed her hand. "Nervous?"

"A little, not because I'm unsure, but just…"

Xander nodded. "You're going to love it."

The next hour flew by as the buzzing of the equipment and the tiny needle stings vibrated through Grace. She shook off the feeling of shame and pushed away the thoughts of *what would Mom think*. Dave finally handed her a mirror and had her stand with her back to the full length mirror on the wall. Grace raised the hand mirror and looked. The red rose was surrounded by redness with the irritation of her skin, but she couldn't take her eyes off the pedals, small, delicate and perfect – absolutely perfect.

"I love it." Grace grinned at Xander. "What do you think?"

"It's perfect for you."

Dave covered it with a gauze bandage, and gave Grace instructions for care for the next two weeks. "If you have questions, feel free to call me or ask Xander. He knows what to do."

"Thanks." Grace pulled out her wallet.

"I got it." Xander threw down cash on the counter. "Always impressed with your work, Dave. Let's get together soon. I'm around for a while."

"You staying at home?" Dave frowned.

"Nope. In a local hotel." Xander was vague and shook his head slightly at Dave. Xander said his goodbye before grabbing Grace's hand and walked her outside. Xander waited for the onslaught of questions from Grace.

"My treat for lunch." Grace looked around. "Where's the best hole in the wall around here?"

"Hole in the wall?"

"Yup, you seem to have a knack of knowing the best places to eat that aren't well advertised."

Xander nodded. "I do. Let's walk. Do you like Italian?"

"Yup."

They strolled hand in hand down the street, stopping every so often to look in windows of stores. They finally came to a small alley off the main street and Xander pulled her in that direction. "This is it."

They stopped in front of a red door in the middle of the alley. A small sign, *Mia's*, indicated the restaurant.

"Wow, this is literally a hole in the wall."

Xander chuckled as he followed her inside.

Chapter Seven

Grace's shoulder ached, but it was a welcome discomfort. She looked at it as a stepping stone to a new life. Secretly she was giddy with the thought that her mom would be furious at her for getting the tattoo. She and Xander had spent the afternoon laughing and chatting over wine and pasta. She had never felt so relaxed. He brought out a carefree spirit in her that she had thought was long gone.

"Okay, Gracie-girl, what else is on your bucket list?"

"What makes you think I have a bucket list?" Grace sipped another glass of wine. She was feeling a little tipsy.

"Don't you?"

She giggled. "You know, I was going to start one last night, but just couldn't bring myself to do it." Where did that come from? She never shared things about herself with others.

Xander sat back and watched her. "So what didn't you write down that you want to do?"

Grace shook her head. "I can't tell you all my secrets, especially when you share nothing about yourself." She raised her glass in toast. "Here's to being mysterious."

Xander clicked his glass against hers. "You no longer want to know who I am?"

"Nope. I don't want to, don't need to. I decided I like just hanging out with you and not having to know or have control over everything."

"And there is a huge thing…Grace lets go of control. I'm shocked." He sat forward. "I'll share something with you. I've always wanted to travel abroad, but found it unappealing to do by myself."

"I understand that. I hate doing things by myself, yet that is the way it always seems to be…me, by myself."

"We should plan to travel, the two of us." Xander played with his water glass, never making eye contact.

"It's Friday. How about we get through the weekend without killing each other and we'll talk about traveling later." She gracefully navigated through the awkward moment. Her heart had sped up at Xander's words. He would be the perfect traveling companion, bringing out her adventurous side and encouraging her to rebel against what she wanted so badly to forget, which was her whole life before meeting him. Her stomach clenched in anticipation as she thought of where the rest of the afternoon would take them. She didn't care where she ended up, as long as Xander was beside her.

They spent the rest of the day wandering the streets, checking out antique shops and just enjoying each other's company. The rain lifted and warmth showered down on them as the sun brightened the sky.

"Why aren't you staying at your home?" Grace asked out of the blue as they headed back to the car.

"It's easier to stay at a hotel. I don't really see eye to eye with my parents."

"Both of your parents are living?"

"Yes. But I was never very close to them. Remember, I was away most of my school years, and never came home after I graduated."

"Do you have siblings?"

Xander stiffened. "Thought you no longer cared about who I was?"

Grace glanced up at him. "I didn't mean to pry."

Xander nodded and swallowed hard. "One brother who I haven't spoken to since I was ten." Xander squeezed her hand. "Let's not talk about this, okay? The day has been too perfect to bring us down."

Grace nodded. "I've got to stop by my mom's house tomorrow. A friend of hers is stopping by to give me some names of people that can help me clean out."

"What do you need cleaned out? I can help so you don't have to hire someone."

Grace stopped next to the car, waiting for Xander to unlock it. "You don't want to do that. It's a mess. Years of accumulation that Mom couldn't be bothered to go through. I have no idea where half the crap came from."

"Come on. You would rather have some stranger helping you than me?"

Grace shook her head. "Not really. I'll call Hattie when I get home and tell her I won't need the names."

"Hattie?"

"Yes. She works for one of the neighbors, I believe. She always came by and visited my mom on her day off. Never missed a week. Even as a child, I remember her always being there. She's a wonderful woman, almost a second mom to me."

Xander swallowed hard. He had to speak to Hattie and ask that she not let Grace know who he was. Grace must hate his family, yet he had no idea that Grace knew Hattie.

Grace sat waiting. "Did you hear me?"

Xander glanced over. "No, I'm sorry."

"I asked if you knew the Stevens in town."

"Yeah, heard of them."

Grace nodded. She sensed it was not a conversation Xander wanted to have, either. She was curious about his past, but enjoyed the freedom of not knowing too much to push it.

"Have you ever been skydiving?" Grace turned in her seat to watch him.

"No, actually I never had. Not sure I would have the courage to rely on a section of fabric to stop me from splattering all over the ground."

Giggling escaped Grace. "I never took you for a coward."

"Coward?"

"Chicken to try?"

"Is that the next thing on your bucket list, Gracie-girl?"

"What's with the Gracie-girl?"

Xander shrugged. "I don't know. I like it."

Grace couldn't help but glow. What was it about a simple nickname that brought a smile to her face and put a song in her heart? Xander had changed her focus in such a short time of knowing him. Was it just the rebellious girl in her that was fighting to get out? She wasn't doing anything too rebellious, but she wanted more from life. Not this mundane, same ol' day after day routine that she had fallen into. She cried out mentally for a new life, one she knew she would never get. One that was only available to her in her dreams.

"What're your plans for tonight?" Xander broke through Grace's thoughts.

"No plans. Probably start that dreaded packing."

"I still don't understand why you have to give up your apartment. Rent the house if you feel the need to keep it."

"I don't have a choice. I will know more after Monday and meeting with the lawyer, but I have a feeling that Mom was up to something, and her will is going to tie me to that house for a while."

"You think she would have tried to control your future that way?" Xander couldn't fathom Abigail pulling a stunt like that. With whatever dealings he had had with her, she seemed so considerate and encourage for him to do his thing. Did she have a double standard when it came to her own child?

"Unfortunately, yes. She gave me a heads up unknowingly when she was begging me to make promises to her that she knew were not in my plans." Grace sighed. "I loved her so much that I couldn't tell her I wouldn't do it…but she knew I found that house suffocating."

"Why?"

Grace glanced at Xander. "Why what?"

"Why is that house suffocating to you?"

Grace shrugged. "It's just…growing up, there were so many happy memories with my dad and mom. After Dad died, Mom changed a bit. She was more depressed, which I know was normal, but it was like the laughter and happiness was gone."

"Hey, at least you had the laughter and happiness. It doesn't mean the house has to be a bad place for you. Make your own memories now…do something in the house to totally change it to fit you."

Grace smiled. "You make it sound so easy."

"No, I know it's not easy. It takes work and sometimes it's hardest to make the changes to something that carries happy memories, but there comes a time where you have to do what is right for you."

"Like you staying away from your family? Never putting down roots?"

The question hit Xander like a ton of bricks. Was that the reason he moved from place to place, because it was too hard to actually stand up to his parents and say what he wanted? Or was it because what he felt was right for him? Xander pulled into Grace's driveway and shut the vehicle off. "I honestly don't know why I live my life the way I do. Rebellion, I guess."

"So when's it time to grow up?" Grace's voice was soft and gentle, like she was talking to one of her second graders. "You give good advice, but I don't think you live it."

"You're right. And I don't have an answer as to why that is." Xander grabbed Grace's hand, lifted it to his lips, and pressed a gentle kiss to the back of her hand.

Grace's stomach fluttered. She watched him, his eyes never leaving hers. His lips caressed her hand, turning it over and kissing her palm. A soft moan escaped Grace. She watched his lips curve into a smile against her hand. "Come in the house," she said and reached for the door handle.

"I really should be going…not that I don't want to, but I want us to take this slow."

Grace nodded. She was grateful for his sentiment, but right now she just wanted to feel those lips everywhere on her body. Her eyes never left Xander's as he leaned close and brushed his lips against hers. She pressed closer, winding her fingers through his hair. Grace felt a loss of heat when Xander pulled away. His breathing was heavy and he closed his eyes to gain control.

Grace watched Xander drive off on his motorcycle and felt the frustration rolling around in her. She had the weekend to pull together packing her apartment before meeting with the lawyer Monday. She needed to stay away from Xander or nothing would get done. She turned towards the house, anxious to remove her bandage and check out her new tattoo.

Chapter Eight

Xander's cell phone started ringing as he drove up to his parent's house. Unknown number. He contemplated ignoring it, but then hit answer. "Xander Stevens."

"Mr. Stevens. This is Bob Rollins. I'm the attorney in charge of the will of Abigail McAllister. Did you know Mrs. McAllister?"

"Yes, sir, I did." Xander glanced at his watch. He was already five minutes late for dinner and his parents were sticklers for punctuality. He shut off the motorcycle, staying seated for the conversation.

"Mr. Stevens, I need for you to stop by my office on Monday, if possible."

"I'm sorry, Mr. Rollins, but what is this all about?" Xander paced on the front porch.

"It's a matter of formality. Mrs. McAllister has named you in her will and I need you here to go over things."

Xander stopped short. "What? That's impossible." Grace was going to have a hemorrhage. What had Abigail been up to?

"Not impossible, Mr. Stevens. Please, can you be here Monday?"

"I'm not sure. Let me call you back. I was supposed to be back at work on Monday." The lie rolled off Xander's lips in desperation to be away from this situation.

"Please, Mr. Stevens, let me know as soon as possible. I can't finalize the will without all parties being aware of what is going on."

Xander promised to call him Monday morning if he couldn't make it, otherwise he would be there. He hauled in a breath, his chest tight with anxiety. He bent over with his hands on his knees, taking slow deep breaths. This was not happening.

Xander slammed the door behind him, striding towards the dining room.

"You're late, Sebastian." His father's voice grated on his last nerve.

"Well, I don't have to stay if it is inconvenient." Xander stood behind the place setting intended for him.

"Sebastian, don't be ridiculous. I'm sure you have a perfectly good reason for keeping us waiting." His mother's voice soothed the situation and Xander felt sorry for her. He pulled out the chair and sat down.

"Apparently, you don't remember that we dress for dinner." His father's snide comment stiffened Xander's back.

"I could have changed, but I would have been even later and figured that would be so inappropriate for you."

Xander met his father's eyes, never wavering. His father broke the eye contact. Although a small victory, Xander knew it would just irritate his father to the point where there would be another confrontation, in private of course.

No confrontation had ever been in front of Xander's mother. John Stevens felt that private confrontation as much more intimidating. Xander could never figure out why would a father want to intimidate his child. Xander's mind went to Grace. She would be a good mother. He could just see it when she talked about her students. She loved children and he knew instinctively that she had more love in her than most mothers showed their children...at least in his experience.

"Sebastian, are you listening to your mother?" John's roar broke through Xander's thoughts.

"Sorry, Mother. What were you saying?"

Elizabeth glanced at her husband. "It was not important, dear."

"Elizabeth, of course it was. Your son needs to pay attention to you when you are talking. He obviously hasn't picked up on how to respect a lady in the room."

Xander sighed softly. "Yes, Mother, please tell me again."

"I was just saying that I hear there were going to be changes at the McAllister home. I'm hoping we will finally get some decent neighbors."

Xander laid his fork down. "What kind of changes?"

"I don't know. I assumed that was going to mean that the daughter would sell the place. She left her mother anyway, obviously didn't want anything to do with her."

"You know that's not true, Mother." Xander stood. "I've had enough of this."

"Where are you going? Sit down, Sebastian." John stood, his fist on the table.

"No, Father. I'm done with this. You think ill of everyone around here. Grace took care of her mother while working full time. So what if she lived in an apartment instead of under Abigail's roof?" Xander took in a deep breath.

"Sebastian. You will not speak to your parents that way. Sit down." John slammed his hand down on the table.

"No." Xander kissed his mother's cheek and headed for the door. He detoured to the back of the house to find Hattie.

"Oh, child, you've gone and done it now." Hattie stood just inside the door, obviously hearing the entire conversation.

"You know it needed to be said. I'm headed out. I'll stop by your place later this week in the evening." He drew Hattie into a hug and held her close. "I love you, Hattie."

"Love you, too, child. Now you go on." She shooed him out the back door.

Xander started his motorcycle and just started riding. The hotel was too oppressing to go to. He longed to go to Grace's, but knew he wasn't in the right frame of mind to see her. He allowed the wind to pull at him as he increased his speed. The fluidity with the bike eased his tension and his focus soon became just on the ride and the enjoyment it brought him.

Xander found himself on the familiar road to Dave's place. He pulled up, relieved when he saw lights on.

He pounded on the door and waited. The door swung open, Dave shaking his head at him. "Dude, you look terrible. Come on it."

"Thanks."

"Beer?"

"Yup." Xander fell into the familiar one-word conversation with his college buddy. Dave was the only one that knew exactly how his childhood had been and the relationship he had with his parents.

"Been visiting the folks?"

"Yup." Xander drained his beer.

"Wow, that good, huh?"

"Man, how did life just get like that for them?

"Okay, let's back up a minute. Who was the hottie you were with today?" Dave handed Xander another beer.

"Grace?"

"Yeah, man. Spill it."

Xander shook his head. "Nothing to tell."

"Bull. I saw the way you looked at her. You are usually a man that is hands off in relationships. The way you two interacted, there's more there than that."

Xander took a swig of his beer. "I don't know. She's different." He peeled the label off his beer bottle. "Remember the old lady that used to write to me?"

"Yeah, the one you said helped you get your act together when you were in trouble."

"Yup, that's her. She died and I went home to the funeral."

"And?" Dave watched Xander.

"She was Grace's mother."

Dave chuckled. "Now this gets interesting. Does Grace know that you were her mother's project?"

"Project? Really? Is that how you look at it?"

"I don't know. You tell me. Was it more than that?"

Xander shook his head. "I don't know, but Grace doesn't know that she was in touch with me; in fact, Grace doesn't know who I really am."

"Man, you've got to tell her."

Xander sat forward. "It gets better." He stood and paced the living room.

"Spill it before you wear a hole in the carpet."

Xander stopped and stared at him. "Apparently I have been named in Abigail's will. I am supposed to go to the reading of the will on Monday. Grace is going to be blindsided by this."

"Shit. You've got to tell her."

"I can't. I'm going to call the lawyer and tell him I can't go."

Dave shook his head at him. "You've got to talk to Grace."

Xander sank into the chair. This was becoming a nightmare. The chest tightness started again and he knew he had to get out of town.

"I know that look, man." Dave grabbed the empty bottle from Xander's hand. "Don't you dare run."

Xander sighed and closed his eyes, laying his head back against the chair. "It's all I know how to do. I've run from years from the hard stuff."

"Let me ask you this. You said Grace was different. Is she worth fighting for?"

"She is."

"So, why are you thinking of running?"

Nothing.

"Well?

"I question if I'm even worth it."

Chapter Nine

Xander spent the weekend with Dave. They had worked on reshingling his roof Saturday, drank that evening and now Sunday was here. They had both avoided the subject of the will and Grace. Xander appreciated his friend's consideration of not bringing the subject up. But time was running out and Xander was no closer to deciding what he was going to do about the meeting with the lawyer tomorrow.

As the afternoon drew to a close, Dave and Xander sat in the shade of Dave's backyard, eating hamburgers and sipping beers. "Whatcha going do?"

Xander grinned. "I knew you would ask eventually. I don't know yet."

"You haven't spoken to her all weekend."

"I know. She probably is upset about that too, but I don't have her phone number."

Dave snorted. "Yeah, and I don't have internet for you to look it up."

"Whatever. You know me."

"I know you usually blow women off, but Grace is different. You're different around her. I saw that in the brief couple of hours I saw you together Friday."

Xander glanced at Dave. "Do you ever wish you had more?"

"More as in a girlfriend or wife? No way, man. I like the bachelor life."

"I thought I did, too." Xander shook his head. "This conversation is getting to sappy."

They spent the next hour throwing horseshoes and laughing about their college days. As dusk set in, Xander knew he had avoided Grace and the subject of his identity long enough. He started the motorcycle and promised Dave he would stay in touch. He headed the bike towards the town that was beginning to stifle him again. In a blink, the decision flashed through his mind. He would call and not go to the reading of the will. He would ask the lawyer not to mention his name to Grace until they had had a chance to meet. He wanted a meeting without Grace present. He swung into the hotel parking lot, went in and stretched out on the bed. Guilt bombarded him as his thoughts drifted to Grace.

He was wrong to have blown her off all weekend. He sighed and glanced at the clock. It was already ten at night. He couldn't call her now. Xander drifted off to sleep with visions of Grace, her hair flowing on the motorcycle. He could feel her grip his hand as she received the tattoo. She was so open to new adventures, and he was running scared once again.

The sun shone directly into Xander's eyes the next morning. He pulled the pillow over his head and cursed the lack of sleep he had gotten. He dragged himself to the shower. Allowing the hot water to rain over him, he felt the tension easy away. He berated himself for being a coward, knowing he had to call the lawyer this morning and bail on going to the reading of the will. He could almost feel the disapproval from Abigail. Why did he even care? A few letters from a motherly figure and he felt obligated to still make her proud of him. He didn't have that obligation to his own mother-- of course his mother never cared whether he got his act together truly, only that he was an embarrassment to the Stevens' name.

Xander toweled off and got dressed. He headed for the *Daisy's Bakery* to grab some coffee and one of Grace's favorite donuts. After receiving his coffee, he found a quiet spot and pulled out his cell phone. He punched in the lawyer's number. It was just barely eight a.m. Xander hoped that Grace wasn't there yet. He needed to make this lawyer understand why he couldn't be there right now.

"Rollins Law Firm."

Xander cleared his throat. "Mr. Bob Rollins, please."

"May I tell him whose calling?"

"His morning appointment." Xander was purposely vague and was put on hold.

"Grace?" A male voice came on the line.

"No. Mr. Rollins? It's Xander Stevens."

"Mr. Stevens, I take it if you are calling me you aren't coming today to our meeting?" The man's frustration came across the line.

"I'm sorry, Mr. Rollins. I can't get there today, but I have a favor to ask."

"Yes?"

Xander took a deep breath. "I need for you not to tell Grace it's me that you wanted there."

"You are named in the will, Mr. Stevens. Grace has to know that."

Xander took in a deep breath. "Mr. Rollins, are you aware of the feud between our families?"

The silence was so dense that Xander thought he must have lost the call before Mr. Rollins spoke again. "Yes, I'm aware. Abigail was hoping this will would bridge that and repair relationships."

"How on earth did she expect for that to happen?"

"Mr. Stevens, I can't go into details on the phone. You need to be here for the reading of the will. Grace just walked in. I will give her the very basics of the will. Can you be here tomorrow? Just you? Let me do the same for you and then hopefully we can all meet at the end of the week to go over everything together."

"Fine. Please just don't tell her yet it's me."

"Tomorrow, Mr. Stevens, ten a.m. sharp."

Xander agreed and ended the call. He had a reprieve into later in the week. He would need to go see Grace today and feel out how the reading of the will went. Hopefully he could get an idea of what kind of havoc Abigail was about to rain down on both of their lives.

Chapter Ten

Grace walked in to the Rollins Law Firm dragging her feet. Bob Rollins had been a lifelong friend of her mother's. Her stomach had been rumbling all morning, nerves taking over. She hadn't even been able to finish her coffee this morning. *Oh, Mom, what have you done?*

Lillian, Bob's secretary, offered her coffee. Grace declined and sat quietly in a corner chair waiting. When Bob finally came out, the grim look on his face made Grace flinch.

"Morning, Grace. I'm glad *you* could make it."

"Uh oh. Does that mean the other person isn't going to be here?"

Mr. Rollins gestured her into his office. "Not this morning, he's not."

"He?"

Bob sighed. "Grace, this isn't easy for me. Abigail put me in a tough position for this will. God bless your mother, I loved her, but she could be stubborn when she wanted to be. I tried to advise her against this type of setting up of the will, but she insisted it was the best way to go."

"I don't understand. What were her stipulations?"

Bob took a deep breath and started reading the will to Grace. He continued through the basic legalese of it and paused briefly before continuing onto the stipulations. "You and the other party will live in the house together."

Grace pursed her lips, but remained silent.

Bob continued, "The business involving the horses will be started and run successfully for a period of two years."

Grace kept her mouth shut, but clenched her teeth. Horror welled up in her.

"These stipulations must be upheld for a period of two years. If at anytime these conditions are not met, the inheritance is forfeited by both parties and will be donated to charity." Bob placed the papers on the desk and glanced up at Grace.

Grace sat there silently, listening. The tightness in her stomach grew with each word. How could Abigail have done this to her? Shock ripped through her and gave way to fury. Her hands started to shake, but she kept her silence, trying to process it all.

Bob laid down the papers and sat back. "Do you understand this, Grace?"

Grace nodded her head. "Basically, I have to live in her house with a stranger and start a business she wanted, but I don't, and have to do that for two years, or I lose it all?"

Bob sat forward. "I know this seems unreasonable, but Abigail thought she was doing the right thing."

Grace stood and paced the small office. "What am I supposed to do with horses? I don't even like to ride."

"That has to be determined between you and the other party."

"This mystery person?

"I'm sorry. I haven't had a chance to meet with him yet. I will be meeting with him tomorrow. Can you come back on Friday so we can all sit down together and go over this in greater detail?"

Grace sighed. "I don't really have a choice. When do I have to be in the house?"

"You have a bit of time. By September."

Grace nodded and picked up her purse. "Thank you, Bob. I know this isn't your doing."

"I'll see you Friday, ten?"

"I'll be here. And this *other party* better, also."

Grace stormed out of the office and started down the street towards the park. She spied *Daisy's Bakery* and crossed the street. Maybe some comfort food would help her sort this out. She was so intent on her own issues, she saw no one when she entered the bakery. Ordering a cup of coffee and two glazed donuts, she turned to come face to face with Xander.

"Grace."

She swallowed hard. She hadn't heard from him all weekend. She put on a bright smile. "Xander. How are you?"

"Good. Join me?"

Grace slid into a chair. She reached for one of the donuts and took a bite. She closed her eyes and let the freshness of it comfort her. She opened her eyes to catch Xander smirking. "No one enjoys these donuts like you do."

Grace shrugged and took a sip of coffee. She eyed him as she took another bite, waiting for...something from him that would explain the sudden shift in climate between them. The silence was awkward. She finished her second donut and most of her coffee before Xander spoke.

"Look, I feel like I owe you an apology."

"For?" No way was she making this easy for him, not in light of her morning. Damn it, she was itching for a good argument with someone... well, really with Abigail, but since her mom wasn't here Xander would do.

"I went to help Dave this weekend – my friend that did your tattoo."

"I know who Dave is."

"Okay. Well, we shingled his room and...I just feel like I should have let you know I wasn't going to be around, but it was a sporadic decision."

Grace sat back. "Xander, you don't owe me any explanations. We spent a little bit of time together, that's it."

Xander felt like a bucket of cold water had been thrown in his face. "Well, I wanted to talk to you, to see you, but I didn't have your number."

"It's listed." Grace snapped out. "Look, I have things to do. I simply stopped in to get a bit of comfort food before diving into my day."

Xander reached for her hand. "What is it, Grace?"

"Nothing." Grace moved her hand just out of reach. "Look I need to go." Xander watched her walk away, fighting everything in him screaming at him to go after her.

Grace hauled in a breath as she exited *Daisy's*. She blinked rapidly to stop the flow of tears. How could he be so nonchalant about not having her number? He never once asked for it in the times they were together. Guilt flooded Grace as she thought of the passionate kisses they had shared and how her thoughts had been on wanting him to stay with her.

She walked rapidly towards her apartment. Her future was decided for her, now she had to pack. She wondered if her mom had intended for her to quit teaching. There was no way Mom would have made her do that. She knew how much Grace loved her students. But how could she start a business while she worked full time? Or was that what this other heir was supposed to be helping her with?

She wanted to scream out loud in frustration. This week was going to be a tough one to get through with all the unknowns. Grace was a planner; wanted her ducks in a row and this putting off finalizing the will until the other heir came forward was unacceptable in her book. She slowed her steps as she neared her apartment. She needed this week over – needed to make decisions that couldn't be made without all the information.

Grace changed her clothes when she got home and pulled out empty boxes while listening to a rock station on Pandora. Looking around the living room, she decided to start with her bookshelves. She had two floor-to-ceiling bookshelves filled with not only her college books, but her pleasure reading as well. She hadn't realized what a collection she had until she filled four boxes.

Taping the boxes shut, she labeled them and pushed them off to the corner.

She switched her Pandora station for a softer rock. Grabbing a glass of wine, not caring that it was only noontime, she slipped onto the sofa and pondered her seemingly bare room. The books had embodied the living room; it was the essence of her life. Her mother had given her a love for reading when Grace was quite young. They had spent hours with her mom reading to her each night. As Grace had started reading on her own, her book collection grew and she spent most of her waking moments with her nose in a book.

Grace sipped her wine and contemplated where she would be in a year. Stuck in the mansion where she grew up, sharing a house and a business with some stranger. She groaned and closed her eyes. This was not going to be good. Two years she would have to run this business with a stranger before she could gain her full inheritance and then decide for herself what to do with the property.

She was pulled from her self-pity party with a knock on the door. It was a tentative knock. She set her wine glass down and moved to swing open the door only to face Xander.

"Hey." His eyes searched her face.

Grace sighed and moved aside for him to enter. "What are you doing here?"

"I needed to see you." Xander stepped into the living room, taking in the packed boxes in the corner. "What's this?"

"Packing."

"Well, that I can see. Why?"

Grace slipped back onto the couch and finished her wine. "Had the reading of the will today. Apparently I need to move back to that monstrosity of a house and live there for the next two years. Need to start a business too."

"What kind of business?"

"Not sure yet." Grace gestured for Xander to sit. She was quiet as he settled on the couch next to her, his arm resting behind her. His fingers played with her hair in her ponytail. "Apparently there is another heir who has yet to be named."

Xander stilled. "What do you mean?"

Grace glanced up at him. "Mom pulled a fast one. She named someone else as a co-heir, but the lawyer won't give me the name until he has a chance to meet with him."

Xander relaxed. "When will that happen?"

"Tomorrow, I guess. We're all supposed to meet on Friday to hear the details of everything." Grace laid her head on Xander's shoulder. She felt safe with him close and she liked that feeling. This was something she didn't want to change in the next year, yet Xander already told her he didn't set down roots. He moved on frequently. Why would she think it would be any different because he was here with her?

"No clue as to the details or who it is, though?"

"None."

"When do you have to move by?" Xander brushed his lips against the top of her head.

"September first. Just figured I would get a jump on the packing. I'm going to have to clean out Mom's before I can move things in." Grace snuggled closer. "If I have to be there, I need to pack away Mom's things first."

"Do you want some help?" Xander wrapped his arm around her shoulder.

"Only if you're going to be around." Grace dreaded hearing Xander say he was moving on, but he made no comment and just pulled her closer.

Chapter Eleven

Xander sat in silence. He didn't want to make promises to Grace he couldn't keep. Would he be able to stay here for two years with her? What happened to her inheritance if he didn't stick around? Would she be penalized also? His mind whirled with the possibilities of what could be with Grace and him, if she could stand him after she found out he was the co-heir to Abigail's estate.

He just wanted to fold her in his arms and keep her there, keep her safe from all the unknowns that were coming her way. He needed to think of something else. "What's next on your bucket list?"

"I'm not sure. There's some traveling…although I've been thinking what it would be like to get my motorcycle license."

Xander chuckled. "Really?"

"Yeah. You don't think I could?"

"Of course you could. If you want to do it, then do it." Xander smiled. "Just because you get your license doesn't mean you have to get a bike."

"But what if I did want a bike?"

Xander shrugged. "I prefer you riding behind me, but if you want a bike I would support it."

"You prefer me riding behind you?" Grace looked up and met Xander's eyes.

He lowered his head so his mouth hovered right above hers. "Yes, nestled between your thighs, your arms wrapped tight around me." He brushed her lips with his before she could speak. Her soft moan brought his fingers into her hair, angling her head to deepen the kiss. His tongue stroked hers slowly.

He broke off the kiss and watched her open her eyes. The hazel had turned to a soft green, a change he had noticed that matched her passion. He cleared his throat and moved back, holding her close to his chest. "Grace, I need to go."

"You don't need to." She ran her hand along his chest.

"I do. It's been a trying day for you. I can't take advantage of that." He moved her gently from him and stood.

Grace rose beside him. She was at a loss of words. She wanted him more than anything. He opened the door with his provocative statement and felt like she had been hit with cold water when he pushed away from her.

He cupped her chin and kissed her softly. "Don't be mad. I feel just as much desire as you do."

She nodded and watched him walk out of the apartment. She sank back into the couch cushion and wished he was still there. He was right, there was too much uncertainty in her life right now and she felt vulnerable. Damn him for being a gentleman when all she wanted to do was being a rebel and act out against the mold Mom had put her in—always the good girl, always doing the right thing.

Grace poured herself another glass of wine. She turned off Pandora and turned on the TV. Flipping through channels, she came to a sappy romantic comedy. Settling into the couch with her wine, she allowed herself to be drawn into the story where there was always a happy ever after.

Xander rode right past the hotel. It was going to be a long night, one he didn't look forward to spending alone. Instead, he chose to ride out to the McAllister homestead. He drove past his parents' driveway and continued into the drive hidden by shrubs that were long due for a trim. He drove slowly down it and parked before the mansion. Whereas his parents' home was cold and gaudy, Abigail's home was inviting. The paint had chipped, but the front porch, with its overstuffed wicker chairs and a swing, invited people to just come up and gather for great times. He could see children running all over this place. Whose children? His and Grace's? It warmed him to think of Grace that way. He could see her petite form showing the bulge of a child within.

He shook his head. He had to get these thoughts out of his mind. She was going to be furious with him by the end of the week when she found out it was him that Abigail left her legacy to share with Grace. What was Abigail thinking? She had to have known how all parties would feel about this! God, his parents would have a hemorrhage.

Xander turned his bike towards the back road that he knew cut between his parents' home and Abigail's, heading towards Hattie's house. She hadn't been able to finish her story about the feud and he was dying to have some insight before meeting with the lawyer. He shut off his bike and watched the TV flicker through Hattie's window. He had such fond memories of spending time here. Hattie had been the comfort he needed when his parents couldn't give it to him. He never understood so much in his life. Why did his brother leave when Xander was so young? He never heard from Dale, but yet he never tried to reach out to him, either. Where was the family that Xander's friends all had? He had spent his youth growing up being so envious of his friends and what they had.

Xander looked up and saw Hattie standing in the door. He slipped off his bike and moved past her into the living room. "Something on your mind, child?" Hattie sank into her rocking chair.

"You got interrupted the other day and I want to know about the feud." Xander sat on the edge of the couch cushion. His stomach clenched with anxiousness, almost fearful of what he might hear.

"It was a long time ago, something that should just be forgotten by now." Hattie rocked back and forth, the squeak grating on Xander's nerves.

"But it's not forgotten and I need to know." Xander closed his eyes. "Hattie, everything is changing."

"Change isn't a bad thing." Hattie shut the TV off. "You know you have always been resistant to change, even as a child. You had a hard time. Gawd, the way you cried when you were going to boarding school."

"Why, Hattie? Why did they send me away?" Xander pleaded.

"Because of Grace." Hattie's matter of fact answer took him back.

"Grace?"

Hattie nodded. "You had a crush on her, wanted to date her. Your daddy found out and sent you away."

"I remember him telling me I would never be with Grace. Why though?"

"I'm not privy to the why's of your family, child."

Xander chuckled. "You know more than you are privy to; you and I both know that."

"Shush, child." Hattie smiled. "I don't know the full story. I do know there was talk about your momma getting pregnant with Dale before her and your daddy was married."

"Why would that cause a feud?"

"It wasn't the reason for the feud. It just was a continuation of fight that had been going on for years." Hattie rocked and Xander sat quietly waiting. "I'm not sure what generation started it, but I know it has gone on and on for years."

"Why make a big deal of me wanting to date Grace though? I was a teenager. Not a relationship that probably would have gone the distance." The words sounded empty even to Xander. He wanted nothing more than for it to go the distance now. He wasn't sure where those thoughts came from, but without a doubt he was starting to fall in love with her.

"Child, you know the best one to ask is your daddy."

Xander shook his head. "That's not going to happen. He was upset that I went to Abigail's funeral."

"So what else is changing?"

Xander fidgeted, keeping his eyes downcast. "Abigail named me as co-heir in her will. Grace doesn't know it yet and I'll get the details this week at the lawyers, but…she's going to hate me."

Hattie sat forward in her rocking chair. "She doesn't know it's you?"

"No."

"Why haven't you told her?"

Xander stood and paced the floor. "She's already upset that there is a co-heir and the stipulations that Abigail put on it. Hattie, it's going to be a mess and I just, I just want Grace to be open to getting to know me."

"Ahh, that says it all right there. Boy, you're ready to settle down finally." It wasn't a question. Hattie could always see right through Xander and she had listened to him talk before he was sent away. The memories came flooding back and suddenly Xander remembered how badly he had wanted to date Grace back then. She had been oblivious to him, so it seemed. Even now, Grace had stated she didn't remember the Stevens boys. Of course, Dale had been sent off years before Xander had.

"Wait. If I was sent away because of Grace, then why was Dale sent away?"

"He was a reminder to your daddy of why he married your momma. He did the right thing, and what your grandfather told him to do. I think you need to talk to Grace before you learn more of this feud. I think it would do you both good to hear it together." Hattie nodded, convincing herself.

Xander sighed. "Thanks, Hattie." He bent over and kissed her cheek. "I'll be in touch."

Xander took the back road to get to town and the hotel. His mind churned with different scenarios of how Grace was going to handle the news.

Chapter Twelve

Xander sat at *Daisy's Bakery*, his coffee cooling in front of him as he stared out the window. He had no idea what to expect at the lawyer's this morning, but one thing was for sure, he knew he'd be expected to move back to this small town. The thought of it choked him, his body screaming at him to run and get away before this meeting.

Expectations. Damn, that word again. Abigail had gone and put expectations on both Grace and him. Expectations that no doubt they would both fail to meet. He shook his head to clear the thoughts. He sipped his coffee and grimaced. Nothing worse than a cold brew. The inevitable loomed before him and he stood. Squaring his shoulders, he walked down the block to the lawyers. Might as well get this over with.

Xander paused just inside the door of the lawyer's office. The secretary talked quietly on the phone, motioning for him to sit down. Xander sank into a chair and tapped his fingers on his thigh. Agitation welled up in him.

"Mr. Stevens, come on in."

Xander rose and passed by the lawyer into the office. He glanced around, taking in the pictures of the man's family. How happy and close they seemed felt like a sucker punch to the gut.

"Have a seat." Bob gestured to the chair. "I'm sure you have lots of questions and Abigail warned me you would not be an easy one to get in here. Thank you for coming."

Xander sat and nodded, then waited for the lawyer to continue. Bob shuffled the papers in a folder in front of him, his hand coming to rest on an envelope. Bob slid it across the desk towards Xander.

"What's that?" Xander made no effort to pick it up.

"It's an explanation, written by Abigail, that she wished you read before we proceeded any further. She knew that you wouldn't come on the first meeting with Grace, although I'd hoped she would have been wrong on that."

Xander stared at the envelope. "Why don't you just tell me what's in it?"

Bob shook his head. "Abigail insisted you read it before we proceed. I will leave you to go through it." Before Xander could answer, Bob exited the office, shutting the door quietly behind him.

The ticking of the small clock on the corner of the desk taunted Xander as he sat still. He didn't want to read it, but his curiosity won. He picked up the envelope and unsealed it. He took a deep breath, trying to calm his racing heart. He unfolded the letter and sat back.

Dearest Xander,

I know you are probably a bit unhappy with me at the moment, wondering why I would name you in the will. And I would imagine your free spirit is feeling a bit stifled, but please try to understand my reasoning.

I first of all owe you an apology. I knew your father sent you away because of Grace. Deep down, I was angry at John for this and I suppose I started helping you out as part of a dig to him. It certainly didn't continue in that vein as I got to know you. I am in total disagreement with your father's thoughts on you and Grace. I feel you two are made for each other and hence, this is part of the reason for my ultimate plot to bring you two back together.

Already you are feeling uncomfortable about this, and I can only hope it is because you feel Grace will be angry with you and I hope you and her have already connected in some way. I am sure, knowing you, however, that you have not been totally honest with my Gracie about who you are. And my dear, you are a Stevens, but that lineage and their mistakes in life doesn't need to define who it is that you've become. We have talked about this numerous times over the years. You can rise above the snobbery of your family and bring a new legacy with your name. Overcome the feud of years ago. There is so much you and Grace don't know. All I ask is that you go into this with an open mind and an open heart for Gracie.

Xander, I have always been very proud of your accomplishments. Stand tall in all that you do and all that you love. Don't let anyone take that away from you.

My love as always,

Abigail

Xander folded the letter and slid it back into the envelope. He blinked the wetness from his lashes. Abigail had always been his cheerleader, no matter what he wanted to do. She had encouraged him—not only to try new things, but to stand up for himself and what he believed, to not follow the crowd. He sighed as he thought about how he had let her down by just staying away from his family as the easiest way to deal with them instead of standing up for himself to his father.

Xander squared his shoulders as the lawyer entered the room again and quietly closed the door behind him. "I trust you had time to read through the letter?"

Xander nodded. "What am I supposed to do with this information?"

Bob's sympathy rolled over Xander. "It wasn't meant to give you all the information you needed for this endeavor, just an explanation of Abigail's thought process."

Xander shook his head. "Doesn't really do that."

Bob sat back in his chair. "What questions do you have for me? Keep in mind, we should be doing this with Grace here, but I understand the oddity of Abigail's request."

"I'm not sure I understand what it is that Abigail even wants from us. The letter was more of an apology than an explanation."

Bob nodded. "I had no idea what it was she wrote. I encouraged her to give both you and Grace a full explanation; apparently she did not. And the letter she left for Grace, there is strict instructions that Grace can't have it until the two years is up."

"Two years?"

"Mr. Stevens, I can't go over the details today with you. I really need to have you and Grace together to get everything out in the open. We need to do this Friday."

Xander stood. "I have a job I need to return to."

Bob nodded. "Yes, a job that you freelance and really can do from anywhere, isn't that correct?"

With a sigh, Xander nodded. "I'll be here Friday." The tension in Xander's shoulders didn't lessen as he strode down the sidewalk with long strides. He was on edge and just wanting a fight. He decided to go home and see what his father thought of this new development. That should be just the fight he needed to blow off some steam.

Xander headed straight to the hotel to get his motorcycle. Revving the engine, he took off towards the Stevens Estate. He relaxed as the motorcycle soothed his tense muscles and his mind cleared as he became one with the bike. Like always, being on the motorcycle calmed him like nothing else could. He drove by his parents' driveway, heading towards the McAllister place. He stopped on the side of the road and took in the view of the house and surrounding grounds. Could he picture himself living here? Yeah, with Grace…if she could ever get over his lying to her. Was omitting the truth the same as lying?

With a sigh, he turned his bike towards the cold home of his family and knew it was time to let his parents know what was going on. Part of him hoped for a fight about it. He wanted to get to the bottom of what the big secret was between these two families, yet part of him didn't really care anymore, not since he got to know Grace. He just wanted to move past the feud and hopefully they could get past this manipulation that Abigail pulled, but he was doubtful that things would ever be the same between Grace and him again.

Chapter Thirteen

Xander stormed into his parents' home. Not waiting for Gerald to let him in, he stopped just inside the foyer. As he glanced around at the grandiose surroundings, bitter bile made its way to his throat. This was a joke—a façade that he had tried to escape, but now it was time to call it for what it was.

"FATHER, MOTHER." Xander's voice echoed through the vast area. He paced in front of the door, waiting for some sort of response. The longer he waited, the more anger coursed through him.

"What is it, Sebastian? Why are you shouting?" John came down the hall from his study. The look of pure embarrassment that his son would even have the audacity to raise his voice in the house just added fuel to Xander's rage.

"We need to talk, NOW." Xander gestured towards the sitting room. This room was rarely used, as they didn't entertain company.

"Why not come down to my study?" John started to turn.

"No. We're not going to your study. We're going to sit in the formal room over here just to give good form to the epitome of lies that we hide behind." Xander strode into the sitting room, leaving no room for argument. He stood at the fireplace, staring into the firebox, listening to his father instructing Gerald to go get his mother.

"What's this about?" John's voice broke through Xander's thoughts. Xander took a deep breath and turned just as his mother strode into the room.

"Sebastian, what is the meaning of this?"

Xander shook his head. "Oh, please. What is the meaning of this façade of a family we have here?" He didn't wait for an answer. "I came back to town for one reason only—for Abigail McAllister's funeral."

"You mentioned that and we agreed it wasn't to be mentioned again."

"No, Mother. You said it wasn't to be mentioned again. I am here for a while because I have some legal business with Grace and the McAllister Estate. I want to know about the feud that went on."

"That is ancient history and something that just isn't discussed." Elizabeth glanced at John and shook her head.

"Sebastian, you need to let this go."

"No. I have been put into something that is going to change my life and I have a right to know about it." Xander clenched his hands by his side and struggled to rein in the anger he just wanted to spew all over his parents. Parents, who should have been a safety net for him, but instead were nothing but an infernal pain in his side for all his life and he was damn if it was going to effect his relationship with Grace.

"Is this about that girl? I thought we got through to you years ago that she isn't for you." Elizabeth stood. "Sebastian, this discussion is over." She turned and left the room as Xander stared after her.

"Walk away like you always do." Bitterness laced Xander's voice as he called to his retreating mother.

"I don't want it brought up again." John's voice was stern, yet Xander sensed he wanted to say more.

"Why can't you just say what it is?" Xander pleaded with his father. For once, he just wanted to be able to talk with the man instead of feeling constantly inadequate around him.

John shook his head. "I can't, son. Please, let it go for your sake, and your mother's."

Xander groaned in frustration. He turned and strode from the house, still no closer to the truth than he had been when he left the lawyer's office. Frustration sliced threw him and he wanted nothing more than to call Grace and hear her soft voice.

Xander was exhausted. The few hours he had been at his parents' house had mentally wiped him out. He knew he needed to see Grace, but it was going to have to wait until tomorrow. He couldn't take anymore. He collapsed on the bed. Abigail certainly had turned everyone's lives upside down.

He dreaded the conversation he would be having tomorrow with Grace. His gut told him this could be the end. He was a Stevens and she was a McAllister, never a good combination and never in history had they ever been together. Xander stared at the ceiling, drifting off to sleep with thoughts of Grace and what could be if they had a future together.

Grace sat out on her balcony. She watched the stars and mentally found the different constellations that she could remember, the little dipper, the big dipper, Orion's belt. She sighed, having hoped Xander would've been by today. He said he had business to tend to; maybe it had taken all day. Uneasiness sat in her stomach like a lead ball.

Ever since Xander had wandered into Grace's life, she had been off balance. Her whole life as she had known it was suddenly tipped over and she craved more. More from Xander, more from herself. Never in her life had she felt so alive as she did when Xander was with her. *Oh, Mom, I wish you were here to talk to. You'd like Xander.* Grace closed her eyes and let a peace wash over her as she allowed memories of heart to heart talks she had had with her mom over the years. She allowed the past words of wisdom to wash over her. Her mom had always told her to follow her heart, but not to allow her heart to be walked on. Grace never fully understood the sentiment until she had had a bad relationship. She realized she had allowed her heart to be a doormat to just keep the peace. She had finally broken it off and her mom had applauded her even through Grace's tears.

Grace had never shed tears for a loss of love, but for the loss of a love she thought she would never find. A hope had come into town when Xander showed up. Grace felt sure the future could be bright as long as Xander was in her life. She allowed herself to drift off to what-if land, one in which a future would be possible with Xander. She mentally kicked herself for not following through on that conversation with Mrs. Smythe as to who Xander really was, but she had convinced herself that it didn't matter. But how long could it go on like that, or would it eventually become an obsession with her?

Grace wished she had the courage to contact him herself.

Chapter Fourteen

Xander woke feeling like a freight train had hit him. His eyes were heavy and he lay in bed wishing he could just die...anything but have this meeting this morning with Grace and the lawyer. He willed his mind to shut down and not overthink everything that could happen at this meeting. Grace was going to be livid when she found out he was a Stevens.

He never went by Xander until he had gotten to college. Grace would've remembered him as

Sebastian if she even remembered him at all. He swung his feet over the side of the bed and rubbed his eyes. Coffee. He needed coffee to get through this meeting.

Showering quickly, Xander put aside his thoughts and focused on the fresh-brewed morning glory he was about to experience at *Daisy's*. He was thinking like a child, but he couldn't dwell on the meeting. Abigail sure threw him under the bus and uprooted his life. He wanted to be angry, yet he couldn't help but worry more about Grace in all this. She was going to be blindsided and he was a coward for not talking to her the past couple of days.

Xander wandered down the street to the coffee shop. He would be arriving early at the lawyer's, but he just wanted it over with. And in his mind he believed that arriving before Grace would give him the upper hand. What did he need the upper hand for? No idea, but it sounded good.

He grabbed his coffee and started down the street for the lawyer's office. He kept an eye out for

Grace, hoping she wasn't one of these that were perpetually early to everything. As he slipped inside, he took the cover off his travel cup and inhaled the rich aroma. The scent immediately cleared his mind and his shoulders relaxed. The tension lessened and he inhaled deeply again.

"Mr. Stevens, welcome. Thank you for coming in." Bob extended his hand.

Xander covered his coffee and gripped the lawyer's hand. Bob gestured him to enter the office.

"Grace should be here shortly." Xander nodded and sipped his coffee. "I know you are worried about all of this, but I think it will be fine."

Xander's mind wandered as Bob rattled on, spouting reassurances that were as empty as Abigail's house at the moment. He sighed. A house he would soon be moving into. He grimaced with the thought of moving into the home with Grace if she absolutely hated him. He prayed for a slight crack in the anger that may come, where an opportunity for healing and a chance for their love to foster might present itself *Their love?* Xander heard the secretary and knew instantly Grace had arrived.

He moved to the back corner of the room, leaning against the wall, causally sipping his coffee and giving the appearance of not having a care in the world. Instead, his insides twisted painfully with the thought of facing Grace.

Grace swept into the office. "Bob, so sorry I'm a few minutes late."

Bob chuckled. "As usual Grace, you are right on time."

Xander took in the jeans and silk top Grace wore. She had her hair pulled back into a ponytail that made her look years younger. He took a tentative step forward. "Grace."

Xander felt like he had just been sucker punched as Grace turned to look at him. "Xander?" Her voice questioned the sight of him, yet her eyes clouded over. "I don't understand. Why are you...?" Grace shifted her eyes between Bob and Xander.

Bob glanced up and smiled. "Grace, you know Sebastian?"

"Sebastian? No, Xander."

Xander glanced down at his now cold coffee. "Sebastian Alexander Stevens. I started going by Xander in college."

"Stevens?" The shrill reached Grace's ears and she cringed. She was not the type to give into hysterics, but no, this just couldn't be. "Why didn't you tell me?"

"I didn't want this reaction. I didn't know what Abigail had done."

Grace stood and walked behind her chair. She gripped the back of the seat and leaned forward. "I point blank asked you your last name, you refused to tell me. You lied to me."

"I didn't lie. I didn't want this reaction and honestly I didn't think I would be sitting here with you right now in this situation." Xander stood. "Please, Grace, sit back down."

"No. There is some mistake." She turned her eyes to Bob. "Tell me this is a mistake. You know the history."

Bob shook his head slowly. "Your mom knew exactly what she was doing, Grace. I'm sorry."

Grace shook her head and closed her eyes. In a matter of seconds, her mother had ripped the rug right out from under her and she had no idea what to do. She needed air. She had to leave. "I need to...I can't do this." Grace turned towards the door.

Xander beat her to it. He placed his hand under her elbow. "Grace, what do you need?" His voice was low. She felt lightheaded and felt like she would collapse at any minute.

"I need you to leave." She hissed at him, but she didn't pull away.

"Bob, give us just a couple of minutes, please." Xander glanced over his shoulder. Xander pulled Grace to the side as Bob left the room, shutting the door quietly behind him.

"No, Xander...Sebastian, whatever your name is. You lied. I can't do this."

"I didn't really lie. I do go by Xander. The only ones that call me Sebastian are my parents. I know this was the last thing you were expecting, but I didn't know about this. I have been just as floored as you to find out about this."

"You knew the other night, didn't you? When I was telling you about my meeting here Monday." The accusation hit him hard and he nodded his head.

"I just found out the night before. I couldn't come Monday. I didn't know what to say to you…I still don't. All I know is I want you in my life, Grace. I want to continue to get to know you."

Grace gave a bitter laugh. "Well, looks like we're stuck with each other for the next couple of years, whether we want to be or not." She walked to the door and flung it open. "Bob, let's get this over with."

She never glanced at Xander the rest of the meeting as they sat and listened to the terms of the will. Xander never took his eyes off her, and she never took her eyes off the lawyer.

"What happens if I refuse to follow these terms?" Xander finally spoke.

"Abigail was very clear. If one of you refuses, the house will be auctioned off and all proceeds will go to charity."

Grace gasped. A tear ran down her cheek. She turned towards Xander. "Well, here's your chance. Your family will be relieved that the McAllisters are no longer their neighbors."

Xander shook his head. "I'm not doing that. Grace, it was a question to see what the results were. I would never have you lose your home."

"It's not my home…well, I guess it is, but it's not what I wanted." She turned towards the lawyer. "What happens at the end of two years, and are there any other stipulations we need to know?"

Oh, Abigail, you did not think this through. I hope this doesn't backfire and you end driving these two apart. "You need to live in the house for two years, together, and start the business of your choice involving the horses that Abigail had already purchased. If either of you don't make it the two years, the consequence I mentioned before goes into effect. There is only one other way to get out of it, but I'm prohibited to tell you that yet."

"Why?" The single word was out of both Grace and Xander's mouths in unison.

"You will need to meet with me every six months, and only then can I give you that information if I see what I need to in order to give you the clause."

"Is there anything else?" Tiredness laced Grace's voice.

"No, that's it. You should move in as soon as possible, but you have until September first. However, the sooner you move in, the sooner the two year time frame starts." Bob stood and shook both of their hands. "Grace, I know this is a shock. Know that your mom loved you very much and she truly thought she was doing what was best."

"If you say so. At this moment, you couldn't convince me of that." Grace turned and left the room, feeling the stares of Xander and the lawyer following after her.

"Thank you, sir." Xander shook Bob's hand again and followed Grace.

By the time he exited the office, Grace was half way down the block. He broke into a jog to catch up. "Grace."

She slowed, but didn't turn towards him. He fell into step beside her. He longed to reach for her hand, lace his fingers through hers and tell her it was going to be okay.

"You're a coward."

"Excuse me?"

"You could have told me; instead, you avoided me the past couple of days."

"I know." Xander grabbed her hand and stopped, giving her no choice but to stop also. "Grace, we need to talk about this."

She pulled her hand free. "No, we don't. You've got your keys to the house. Pick a room on the west side of the house, I'll be on the east side. We will have nothing to do with each other over the next couple of years except for any conversation that Mom has dictated by her agreements. Understood?"

Xander searched her eyes and the flames burning there cautioned him against saying anything. He simply nodded and watched her walk away. It was going to be a long two years if they weren't talking.

Chapter Fifteen

Grace taped up the last box she had filled. Her apartment was empty except for the boxes she had to take to the car. She was moving back home. She didn't know when Xander would be arriving to the house, but she didn't care at this point. She just wanted to get these crappy next two years over with. She glanced around her apartment. Celia, one of her good friends, had agreed to sublet the apartment from her so she wouldn't have to give it up.

She lugged the rest of the boxes to the car. She leaned against the car and just looked at the apartment. She had loved this place; her mom knew that. She was so angry she couldn't even shed a tear at the way her life had been manipulated. She felt the bitterness creep into her and that angered her, too. Bitter was the last thing she wanted to be feeling. Just a week ago, she was letting go of her inhibitions, getting a tattoo with Xander...

Xander, the man she felt most alive around and now the man she absolutely detested so much she couldn't see straight.

Sebastian. She remembered him from grade school. He had been a year ahead of her and she had thought he was so good looking. Well, he hadn't lost his looks. She sighed. She had wanted him to ask her out so badly and her mom had talked with her about him at length. She had said he wasn't for her, that she needed to set her eyes on someone better suited for her. Grace had been heartbroken when Sebastian went away. She never heard another word about him. It was like he had dropped off the face of the earth.

Time to start over one more time, on someone else's terms. She hoped Xander felt as out of control as she did. She couldn't handle if he took this all in stride. She needed him off kilter as much as she was so at least they would be on even ground.

By the time Grace turned into the driveway of the house, her nerves were frazzled. She didn't want to run into Xander. Yet all she could think about was falling into his arms and letting him hold her, telling her it would be okay. She turned off the car and just sat there, staring.

She had so many memories here. Most good ones. She loved growing up here, but had always longed to be out on her own. Well, she certainly was on her own now, just not the way she envisioned it. She sighed as the front door opened and Xander stepped out. He had beat her here.

She watched him descend the steps slowly before she opened the door as he reached her car. "Need some help?"

Grace nodded and popped the trunk open. "Did you get settled in okay?"

"Yup. Took the room farthest away from where you will be." He grabbed a stack of boxes and headed inside.

She had been wretched to him and here he was thinking of her comfort and not trying to invade her space too much. Grace sighed as she watched Xander go into the house, arms full of boxes. She regretted what she had said to him, but there was no doubt about it, this was a difficult situation at best. She had come to the conclusion last night as she tossed and turned in her bed that it would be best to stop anything between them now.

They spent the rest of the morning in silence, lugging in Grace's stuff. Xander quietly disappeared while Grace started to unpack. She surveyed the room. Nothing had changed since she moved out five years ago. Her old accomplishments, trophies, and certificates filled the bookcases and hung on the wall. The room was a room of a teenager and Grace hated it.

She wandered down the hall to what had been her mom's room. There had been many nights Grace had slept in here beside her mother, caring for her. The room had been cleaned thoroughly after her death. She sat in the reading chair beside the bed and closed her eyes. Memories of her mom and dad, laughing and dancing with her, filled her mind. How she wanted to be mad at her mother for doing this to her, yet love overcame the resentment that Grace tried so hard to hold onto the past few days.

Xander wandered around the kitchen familiarizing himself. The refrigerator sat empty. He started a list of what they would need for basics. He took the stairs two at a time looking for Grace. Her room was empty. He moseyed down the hall and peeked in another room. She sat in a chair, eyes closed, a small smile on her face.

Xander leaned against the doorframe and just wanted her. Although her hair was pulled back once again, she looked so peaceful and beautiful. Grace had no idea how beautiful she was, inside and out. She was someone in this short time that Xander had found himself looking up to. She wanted more in life, but saw the good in everyone. He could only hope she would see the good in him over the next couple of years.

He cleared his throat softly. "Grace?"

Her eyes opened slowly. "I can't do it. I can't move into my old room."

Xander approached her and kneeled before her. "Then don't. Take a different room. Sleep in here."

Grace shook her head. "No. This was Mom's room."

"I get that, but she's gone, Grace. This is your house now. Make it yours."

Grace smiled. She squeezed Xander's hand. "Our house now, apparently." It was a simple statement, no anger, no bitterness, just fact.

"I'm headed to the store to get some provisions. Do you want anything special?" Xander stood.

"Do you want some company?" Grace looked up at him. He was all muscle and she remembered the feel of those arms wrapped around her, his lips touching hers. She ran her tongue over her lip.

"Sure, but we can only get limited things with the bike."

"We'll take the car and stock up." Grace stood as Xander took a step back. "Give me two seconds."

Xander waited downstairs in the living room. He took in the pictures on the mantel and the braided rug on the floor. So outdated. The pictures weren't bad, but they were all of Grace as a child. He somehow had to get Grace to accept the fact that she needed to make changes around here to make this place hers. Granted, she had only been here a matter of hours so far, but for the next two years,

Xander didn't wanted to be looking at Grace's childhood. He wanted her future.

"Ready?" Grace spoke behind him.

"Yup." He gestured for her to go before him as they headed out the door.

The car ride was silent. Xander pondered how to bring up the fact that they needed to make the house their own. He didn't want to step on Grace's toes, but he had seen the effect of her mother's room on her. She needed to not be in her childhood bedroom and take ownership of the house.

"Penny for your thoughts?" The silent was broken with the quietness of Grace's question.

"You sure you can afford that?" Xander smiled.

"Are they worth it?" Grace bantered.

"Not really." Xander shrugged. "I just wondered how you were going to make this house yours?"

"What do you mean?"

"Well, you're not a child back at home. This is your house. Don't stay in your childhood room, but change the décor, do something to make it yours."

Had he offended her? The silence was deafening.

"Well…it's not really my home, is it?"

"Of course it is." Xander stared at her.

"Not technically. It's *ours,* on condition. So I guess if you want to change the décor, you can."

Xander kept silent as Grace parked the car. As soon as they entered the store, Grace immediately bristled. "Look, why don't you get what you want and I will get what I want and then we'll be able to keep everything separate."

Xander grabbed her hand and kept her next to him. "We're not doing this separately, Gracie. We are in this together, for better or for worse."

"It's not a marriage, for God's sake. It's a manipulation that Mom pulled and we have no choice."

Xander pulled her outside. "Come on. Let's walk."

Grace hesitated for a second before falling into step with Xander, her hand still linked with his. They turned away from downtown and headed out a side street. Xander warmed at the feel of Grace's hand in his, feeling positive that she hadn't pulled away from him.

"I'm sorry. It's not you." Grace whispered.

"I know. We were both blindsided with this. I should have told you who I was, but I enjoyed just being with you too much to ruin that. I never could have imagined that Abigail would have done this to us."

"I am still ticked at you about not telling me who you really are, don't think I'm not, but…I understand it too." Grace squeezed his hand. "I just don't know how things are supposed to be now."

Xander nodded. "How do you want things to be, Gracie?"

"I don't know." Grace stopped. "We really should go get the groceries. There is still so much to do at the house."

"Okay. But this conversation isn't over. Think about what you want."

They shopped in comfortable silence, learning each other's preferences in foods. Grace discovered Xander loved to cook and she deemed him the new chef of the house. By the time they arrived back home and food had been taken care of, they were back to a level of comfortableness between them with easy bantering back and forth.

Chapter Sixteen

The next few weeks flew by as Grace and Xander settled into their new home. There was an easy camaraderie between them. Grace came to enjoy having Xander around the house, but continued to keep her guard up.

Awaking early to find coffee already ready, Grace made her way to the kitchen. "Hey."

"Good morning. Coffee?"

"Absolutely." Grace slid onto a bar stool, smiling as Xander slid a full cup in front of her.

"What's on the agenda today?" Xander leaned against the sink, sipping his coffee.

"We need to find out about this business aspect we have to put into play." Grace played with her mug. "I'm just not sure how we're supposed to go about this."

"Well, Bob said that Abigail had things in the work. Guess the best place to start is with him."

Grace shook her head. "I suppose. I'm so tired of Mom still playing games with my life…well, your life too."

"Let it go. It's two years of our lives and then you can move on and do what you want." Xander rinsed his empty cup and strode from the kitchen. He wanted more than anything to hear Grace decide that she wanted him as part of her life, but he wasn't sure it would happen that way. Two years was a long time for things to change…or not change.

He started outside for the stables. The barn was a new structure on the premises and he wanted to see exactly what Abigail may have been planning. There had to be some sort of clue in the barn. He stopped short a few feet from the building. It was obviously new, probably within the last year or two. He would have to remember to ask Grace exactly when it had been built. There was a place for a sign to hang above the door and the emptiness of it stood out. Sliding open the door, the empty stalls were clean and the whole barn was spotless. Never been used. Xander inhaled the smell of freshly sawn lumber. He closed his eyes and let the scents flow over him. The scent of oil on the hinges added to the newness of the lumber. To the left of the door was a tack room with hooks already installed for bridles and saddles for at least four horses.

Xander moved about the tack room, running his hand over the soft leather of the saddles. These were expensive saddles. Abigail had obviously spared no expense when it came to setting up the barn. He continued further into the barn and toward the stairs that led to the loft. Climbing them, he saw bales of straw already in place.

Just what sort of plan did Abigail have in mind? She had already had things in place. Xander sat down on a bale and stared into space. He had so many questions. And how did he fit into all this? He shook his head to clear his thoughts. He couldn't dwell on this. Abigail had saved his life in more ways than one and he owed her. He intended to see this through even if Grace decided she wanted nothing to do with him at the end of it all.

Xander lay back on the bale and closed his eyes. It seemed a lifetime ago that he had been in such trouble that Abigail had stepped in. He had been running with the wrong crowd, drinking heavily and experimenting with drugs. The night he got arrested and his own father wouldn't come bail him out, Abigail had shown up and told him to get his act together. She had continued to meet with him weekly to hold him accountable for getting schoolwork done and staying out of trouble.

Xander had been devastated when he had been sent to boarding school and had to stop meeting with Abigail. She had been the mother figure that he never had in his life. He had stayed on the path of getting his schoolwork done and finishing college because of the letters he had received from her. He sighed as he thought about that moment when he realized how much love he never had from his own mother and father. They were parents who watched from afar, never hands on and certainly never telling him that he could amount to anything more than the rebellious teen he had become.

His thoughts shifted to Grace and the crush he had on her when he was younger. His father had made it clear he was being sent away because of Grace. Why? What was the big issue with Grace and him getting together? Xander smiled at the thought of what his father would say now if he knew they were living together – well, in the same house, anyway.

"Xander?" Grace's voice broke through his daydreaming.

"Up in the loft." He yelled down.

He sat up and waited for Grace to appear. She held the ladder tightly, white knuckling it, as she ascended into the loft. "What are you doing up here? And where did all those bales come from?"

"I was just thinking, and not sure about these. I'm assuming your mother had something to do with it." He patted the bale next to him for her to join him.

"I always hated being up in the loft. So high." Grace sat beside him.

"I'll carry you down." Xander joked.

"No joke. I might need you to." Grace looked around. "Did you see the saddles downstairs?"

"Yeah. No idea what Abigail was thinking though. I thought maybe I would find a clue out here as to what she had hoped to gain with all this."

Grace sighed and lay back. "If you don't think about the height of this loft, it's pretty cozy up here."

Xander's chuckle brought her gaze to him. "Scared of a little height, Gracie?"

"Why do you do that?" She smiled and closed her eyes.

"What?"

"Call me Gracie."

Xander watched her, taking in the softness of her features with her eyes closed. He ran a finger along her jaw line. "Because it suits you and it makes you smile."

Grace opened her eyes and found Xander's face within inches of hers. "Xander," she whispered.

He lowered his head until his lips met hers. The kiss was gentle and coaxing. She sighed as she responded. Her hands slid up around his neck and pulled him closer. She parted her lips, allowing their tongues to meet, stroking each other. She felt the weight of him as he moved his body, half covering hers. Passion rose between them and in the back of Grace's mind she knew she needed to stop this before it went any further. This was a complication she shouldn't--couldn't--have right now.

She pushed against him, breaking off the kiss. "We can't."

"Grace…" Xander sat up and closed his eyes, breathing deeply to calm the fire in him.

Grace rose and walked quickly to the ladder. "Xander, we can't do this." She disappeared down them and sprinted for the house.

Xander sighed. He had pushed it and now she was mad. Damn Abigail for putting them in this situation to begin with! He should have been able to court her, not struggle with this hanging over them. He stood and headed back to the house. A motorcycle ride to clear his head was just what he needed, and maybe even go see Hattie.

Chapter Seventeen

Grace stared out the window watching Xander race away. She was a fool. She knew the feelings between them were real; she just couldn't get past the fact that he had lied to her. And now this whole living situation…she had no way of getting away from him. Although if the truth be told, she didn't want to be away from him. She wanted to allow herself to fall into his arms and let him love her like she had only dreamt was possible.

She turned from the window and looked around the living room. She was seeing it like she had as a child. There was not one thing in the room that made it hers. This was Mom's living room. How could she take these things, the pictures of her childhood, the memories she had and just pack them up? She sank into her mom's favorite rocking chair. Slowly pushing back and allowing the rocking motion to take over, Grace slipped into her childhood memories. She had had a great childhood. Her parents loved her and each other. Their house was one that Grace had always felt safe in. Why couldn't she have that back?

She longed to relive that happiness again. Not just floating through life and hoping the right one came alone, but actively participate in her life and find the one that made her smile and laugh. Or had she already found him?

Grace stood with renewed determination and headed for the basement in search of an empty box. It was time to start fresh and stop living in the shadow of her mother. Grace flipped on the light switch and glanced around. The basement wasn't a spot she visited much growing up. She disliked the cold dampness as well as the shadows that lined the walls. It was creepy and chills ran down her spine.

She moved to the far wall where boxes were lined up. Each box was clearly marked "Christmas Decorations", "Vinyl Records", etc. Grace shifted a few boxes to the side and came across a small shoe box held closed with rubber bands. There was no marking on the box. Grace pulled the bands off and opened the cover. Inside were letters, some held together with rubber bands, others loose, yet all were yellowed with age and addressed to Abigail. There were no return addresses, but the post marks of the most recent top ones were from years ago when Grace had been just a baby.

Holding the box, she started back upstairs. She was intrigued and dying to know who would have written her mother. Were they love letters from her father from the time he was away? He had for years had a job that took him traveling for extended periods. How sweet to think her dad had written to her mom all those times.

She sank back into the rocking chair and flipped through the letters, looking for the oldest one. Pulling it out from the envelope, she sat back, rocking slowly. She didn't recognize the writing. She immediately went to the signature at the end of the letter. Seeing "All my love, John" threw her. Who was John?

She closed her eyes and took a deep breath. Ready to read, she opened her eyes and focused. The date was a few years before she was born. Whoever John was, he had been deeply in love with Abigail. He talked about how much he missed her when they were apart and how much he worked to right things so they could be together. Right what? What kept them apart? Grace read letter after letter, sympathy welling up in her for the agony that this John felt in being apart from her mother. She could only assume her mother felt the same way. The only comments that gave her those indications were the comments John made in response to things Abigail must have written in letters to him.

She turned the letters and envelopes over and over, searching for some clue as to where they had been mailed from. No return address. The postmark was from the closest city to their small town, where all the mail came from. John could have lived in this same town, or a few towns away, and there was no way to tell.

Grace heard the door open and she stopped rocking, folding the last letter back into the envelope before slipping it into the box. She closed up the box and slid it onto the floor beside her just as Xander strode into the living room.

"Nice ride?"

Xander stopped when he saw her. "Yeah, it was good." He sat on the edge of the couch. "I stopped and saw Bob. He sent this packet for you regarding the business that Abigail had in mind for us."

Grace nodded, but made no effort to reach for the manila envelope.

"You okay?" The concern in Xander's voice brought Grace's eyes to meet his.

"Yup, of course. I think we need to stick to the business and just get through the next two years." Grace picked up the shoe box and stood.

"Grace, we should talk about this. One minute you're open to things and the next you're closed off. What's going on?"

"There is nothing to talk about. We are business partners, nothing more." Grace turned and left the room, leaving Xander staring after her. She hurried up the stairs and slammed her bedroom door shut. It wasn't fair to Xander that she was so all over the place, but she couldn't stay in the same room with him without his charm working on her. She needed to protect herself at all costs, and right now she just wanted to figure out this new secret from her mother's past. John…who was he and where did he fit into her mother's life?

Xander sat back down on the couch. What the hell was the matter with her? Had he really screwed it up so badly that she couldn't even look at the business venture? He pulled out the papers from the envelope and read through them. Plain and simple.

Abigail had purchased four horses that had been trained in therapeutic riding for special needs children. They were to open a business using these horses to provide therapy riding for autistic children, or any other child with sensory needs. There were clear instructions as to where the horses were and who their stable manager was. Xander was to market the business and Grace was to run the financial end of it.

It could work, Xander thought. It was a sound plan and there was a need for it, from what he had read in Abigail's business plan. Grace needed to be onboard, but she was a teacher of young children. Xander had no doubt that this idea would warm her and allow her to still interact with those children she loved so much. And he was convinced that she should be able to continue to teach while they worked on this business together.

He threw the papers on the coffee table and headed to the kitchen. They could talk about this over dinner, and what a dinner he would plan for her. Damn it, he was going to court her whether she wanted it or not. He wasn't giving up that easy.

The next few hours, Xander devoted himself to cooking. By the time dinner rolled around, the smell of chicken parmesan, garlic bread and pasta filled the house. He had even made a chocolate cake for dessert. With music blasting, Xander moved around the kitchen singing along softly and moving to the beat.

"Well, well, this is quite the scene." Grace leaned against the doorframe.

"How long have you been there?" Xander grinned.

"Long enough to know that, from the smell of things, you cook better than you sing and dance."

"Hey, I could serenade you and you would swoon."

Grace laughed. "In your dreams, buddy."

"Should we wager a little bet on that?" Xander's eyes twinkled, but seriousness oozed off him.

"No thanks. I will be happy though to eat whatever Chef Xander makes." Grace slid onto a bar stool. "It seems delicious. Is that chocolate?" She pointed to the cake.

"Yes, your favorite I believe."

"How would you know that?"

Xander shrugged. "I used the recipe labeled Grace's favorite."

"Mom's recipe. Oh, definitely my favorite." She reached to swipe some frosting. Licking her finger, she closed her eyes and sighed. "Heavenly. When do we eat?"

Xander shook his head. "As soon as you set the table."

The banter continued as Grace set the table and Xander put the finishing touches on the food. Finally sitting down, Xander waited until Grace was well into her meal before putting the business plan before her.

"We have to talk about this, Gracie."

Grace glanced at him. "Why ruin a good meal with that?"

"It's a good plan your mom had. Read it over while you eat." Xander continued to eat, ignoring Grace. Out of the corner of his eye, he saw her place the papers where she could read them. They finished their meal in silence.

Xander cleared the plates as Grace continued to read the business plan. "Coffee with cake or a glass of wine?"

"Wine, please." Grace laid the papers aside. "Not talking about this while I'm enjoying my cake." She gave him a look that spoke of no nonsense.

With dishes done and wine glasses refilled, Grace grabbed the papers and gestured for Xander to follow her to the living room. She settled onto the couch with her legs tucked up underneath her, sipping her wine.

Xander sat beside her. Silence filled the air as they both sat with their own thoughts. Grace broke the stillness. "Okay, it's a good plan."

Xander grinned. "Yup."

Grace turned to face him, her leg resting against his thigh. "That's it…yup?"

"Let's hear your thoughts."

Xander took another sip of wine and waited while Grace struggled outwardly with what she wanted to say. The closeness of their bodies clouded her mind, or was it the wine adding to that? She just wanted to kiss him and he sat there acting like the closeness wasn't affecting him.

"Looks like Mom has it all set up. When do we start and what do you need to do for marketing?" Grace took a deep breath. There, it was in his court now. She could just sit back and watch him.

"I can put out flyers and make a web page. There are different venues we can use to advertise – local newspapers, online advertising, schools…we can look into special needs programs and put out the information through them."

Grace nodded. "What do I do during all this?"

Xander locked eyes with her and held her gaze. "Teach."

"What do you mean?"

"Grace, you don't have to give up teaching. You love it and you can still do the financial aspect of this riding business in the evenings or on weekends."

Grace shook her head. "I don't think that is what Mom had in mind."

"Where does it say that Abigail says you have to give up teaching?" Xander let his hand slide over her knee and rested it there. "She's not dictating everything. From what I read, as long as we do the business, you can continue to teach and live your own life."

Grace downed the remainder of the wine in her glass. "What is my life? I don't even know

now." She stood suddenly. "Thanks for dinner, Xander. I'm going to head to bed."

Xander sat there as Grace practically ran from the room. He frowned. She was running from him and he didn't like it one bit. He wanted to kiss her goodnight and let her run if she must, but it would be with thoughts of his lips on hers, his body pressed against hers. Instead the thoughts remained in his mind and he had no idea if she even thought of him.

Chapter Eighteen

Grace paced her bedroom. She was a coward. She yearned for someone to love her like the kind of love she read in the letters to her mom from John. The love was so transparent and strong. Grace pulled out the shoebox and picked up where she had left off. She still hadn't figured out what had kept John and Abigail from being together, something about family, but whose?

Grace read until after midnight. Her eyes felt heavy from the reading of the yellowed papers and the writing that was difficult to decipher at times. She still had no further insight as to who he was, but without a doubt she knew John had been a strong love in her mother's life and obviously before her mom had married her father. The mystery became more mysterious and Grace finally closed her eyes with the letters by her face as she drifted off to sleep.

Her dreams filled with images of her mother and a faceless man running from whatever obstacle they had to face to just be together. Grace awoke shortly after two a.m. with her cheeks wet from tears she had been crying. She put up the letters and crawled into bed. She tried to coax sleep to come to her, but it eluded her and she lay there awake, staring into the darkness with thoughts of Xander and what it would be like if she allowed herself to love him.

She finally flipped on the light. There was only one more letter to read and although she was dreading it, she had a feeling this was the letter that ended it all. She bolstered herself up on her pillows and opened the final letter.

My dearest Abby, I can't tell you how much my heart is breaking at how this is ending for us. I know you feel the pain as much as I do and can only wish that you know how much I want to be there holding you right now. My father has insisted I marry Elizabeth even though I know the child she carries is not mine. There has been no other woman for me but you. My darling Abby, please know you are the only one I will ever love, but that I want you to be able to move forward and find a better love for yourself. Find a man that will give you what I could not give you. I will always be with you, my dear, and you will always be in my heart. I will continue to watch you from afar and know that should you ever need anything, I will be here for her. All my love, John.

Grace cried tears for her mother's loss. How could he have done this to Mom? Was he being truthful and really married someone who bore another man's child simply because his father insisted? Why had this man been such a coward?

Grace tossed and turned the rest of the night. She only had more questions after she had finished reading the letters and needed answers. Her mother had never given any indication of a past love, and she knew from seeing her parents together that they had been very much in love.

After a restless night, Grace woke, feeling like she had been hit by a truck. She stood in the shower with her eyes closed, water raining over her. Her mind raced of the possibilities of her mom's life and this John's, whoever he may be. The place to start was at the lawyer's. Maybe he would know who John was. With a plan forming in her mind, she rushed through her shower and got dressed.

Entering the kitchen, she breathed a sigh of relief that Xander was nowhere to be found. She doctored up her coffee and breathed in the aroma before taking that first sip. Eyes closed, she allowed the richness to wash over her and warm her from the inside out. She took a deep breath and set her cup aside, reaching for the pad of paper on the counter. A list was what she needed to figure this out. She always had been a list person, feeling it kept order to her life when she felt out of control. And a love affair that her mother had had before her father's time, well, that definitely fell into the "out of control" column in Grace's book.

Chapter Nineteen

Grace walked into the house. Her mind still reeled from the information she had uncovered. There had to be only one explanation for this situation she was in with Xander. Abigail had been manipulated instead of her manipulating them. Xander and his father – John, former love of Abigail's, had set this all up to get the McAllister estate. It was all so clear now.

Holding back the anger, Grace made her way from room to room searching for Xander. She was ready for a fight and wanted to have it out right now. Not finding Xander on the first floor, Grace took the stairs two at a time to check out the bedroom area. It was empty also. She growled in frustration.

Deciding there was further need now to check out the basement in more detail, Grace started for the cellar and where she had found the letters between Abigail and John. Arriving in the basement, she glanced around to the boxes where her mom's stuff was packed away. She hadn't gone through half of them, yet they had been strewn all over the place, with things knocked out of the boxes and scattered across the floor. She bent down to start picking them up to repack them.

Why did Xander do this? What was he looking for? She paid no attention to what she picked up as her thoughts drifted to Xander and how much she had fallen for his charm. The disappointment in what she had hoped could have happened between them, the thought of an actual relationship, sliced through her. How could she had been so wrong about him?

"Grace?" Xander's voice brought her back to the present.

"Downstairs." She stood and waited for him to appear, her hands clenched at her side.

"What happened down here?" Xander glanced around, paying no attention to Grace. He bent down to pick up some papers near the stairway.

"Don't touch those." The tone in Grace's voice startled both of them. "Haven't you done enough?"

"What have I done?" Xander took a step back. He searched Grace's face and saw only fury. Her stance was tense and she looked as if she wanted to plummet him. "Grace?"

"Why? Why throw Mom's stuff around like this? Have you no respect?" Tears started running down her cheeks. The sight of those tears was like a fist to Xander's gut.

"Grace, I didn't do this."

"Am I supposed to believe that after....after all you and your *father* have done to manipulate this little set up? How much did it cost you, or Mom, for your father to get his way and go after *my home*?" Her voice raised an octave.

"What are you talking about?" Xander took a step towards her. "What does my father have to do with this?"

"You tell me!" Grace pushed past Xander and ran up the stairs.

"Grace, wait!" Xander glanced back at the mess on the floor and then at the stairs. What the hell had happened this morning while she was gone for her to be in this rage? With a backward glance to the mess, he went after Grace.

Xander found her in the living room, pacing. "Want to tell me what it is you are accusing me of?" Xander sat down on the couch.

"Like you don't know. Why? That's all I want to know. Why did you do it?" Grace wiped the tears away. "You played me for a fool."

Xander sat forward. "What the hell are you talking about? Are you insane?"

Grace stared at him. "Am I *insane*? Am *I* insane?"

"That was the question." Xander stood and walked slowly towards her. "What's going on, Gracie?"

"Don't...don't call me that." She turned and faced the fireplace, taking a deep breath.

Xander wrapped his arms around her waist and pulled her against his chest. He whispered, "Talk to me."

"It was your father." Grace sobbed, the dam bursting in her.

"My father what?" Xander held her close.

"That was Abigail's love...those letters were from him."

Xander's arms around her tightened. "What letters?" He turned Grace to face him. "My father and your mother..."

"You didn't know?" The question of what was the truth hung in the air between them.

Xander shook his head no. "You've got to believe me, Gracie. I didn't know."

Grace shrugged. "I don't know what to believe." She pushed against his chest to move out of his arms.

Xander ran his fingers through his hair. "You know I haven't been around here."

"Yet you had contact with Mom. What am I supposed to believe?" Grace sank onto the couch cushion. "Why seek me out at her funeral? Why?"

"I promised Abigail I would check on you…and then I spent time with you and well, I enjoyed your company. Is that so hard to believe?"

Grace closed her eyes, not even opening them when Xander sat down next to her and took her hands in his. "Grace, you are a wonderful person…beautiful, funny, a joy to be around. You make me relax and want to just celebrate life. I haven't felt that way in a long time."

"This can't happen." Grace pulled her hands away from Xander's. "There is too much at stake here and if you think for one second I'm walking away from Mom's...*my home*, you're wrong."

"God, Grace, I would give it all up in a heartbeat if it would just go to you. The only reason I'm here in this house with you is because of the stipulation that you would lose everything. Well, that and I want to be close to you."

"Why? Why do you need to be here—beyond the stipulation?"

"Stop overthinking it." Xander stood and started for the door. "Take some time...we'll talk later."

Grace raised her hand to stop the words, but she knew he was right. It was a conversation that they had to have and one she dreaded at the same time.

Xander sat on his motorcycle, staring at the house. Why did she push him away at every turn? Why did it hurt so much to think she didn't want him? He was the one that could take or leave any woman that was in his path. He prided himself on the fact that he never got involved with any one woman, but loved his bachelor life…yet, Grace had worked herself into his heart and he couldn't deny that he, for the first time ever, wanted to settle down and see what could become of a life with her.

With a sigh he started the bike, and turned towards his parents' house. Funny, he never considered it his home. It hadn't been since he had been sent away. It was time for answers and apparently his father had more answers that Xander could have ever imagined.

Chapter Twenty

Xander took a deep breath as he approached the front door. He paused before knocking, trying to put his mind in order. The door swung open by Gerard.

"Mister Sebastian? I thought I heard your bike. You're here to see your father?"

"Yeah, Gerry. Is he around?"

Xander smirked as Gerard shuddered, giving Xander a withering look. "In the study, sir."

"Thanks." Xander started down the hall, steps slowing as he came closer to the study. He knocked softly on the door and waited for his father's usual, "Enter".

Xander walked in, partially shutting the door behind him. He approached his father's desk, taking in the law books on shelves behind it, the dark wood making the room gloomy.

"Sebastian, I wasn't expecting you."

Xander nodded and sat down. "Funny, I wasn't expecting to be here, but then I've been hearing some things and I want to know the truth. Think you can be honest for a few minutes?"

John sat back in his chair. He gestured for Xander to continue.

"When did you have a fling with Abigail McAllister?"

"What?"

"Honesty for a change, Dad."

Xander watched his father's expression and the softness come to his features that Xander had never seen before. A smile lit up his face and his eyes gleamed. "Well, Sebastian, I guess it's time you knew."

John stood up and came around the desk to sit in the chair next to Xander. "Abigail was the love of my life. Grace looks a lot like her when Abigail was her age. Sometimes it's hard to see Grace around town, she looks so much like her." His voice was soft as he drifted off into his memories.

"When?"

"Years ago, before your mother and I married."

"What happened?" Xander sat back and waited.

"Your grandfather, well, he didn't feel she was the right class for me." John chuckled. "You know, she could light up a room when she walked in. She was always smiling, laughing at something. She was so beautiful, so full of life."

"I've never seen you filled with so much joy, Dad."

"Xander..." John smiled. "She was so angry at me for calling you Sebastian after you changed it to Xander, did you know that?"

"You still had contact with her? I thought there was a feud?"

John stood. "Let's get a drink."

They walked in silence to the kitchen where John poured himself two fingers of scotch and handed Xander a beer. "It wasn't really a feud. There was a social class difference. It was all very stupid and well, at the time I didn't have the backbone to stand up to my father. Not like you."

"Me? I haven't really ever stood up to you."

John nodded. "You have, subtly. You left and didn't come back. In a way, you were saying you had enough. And I get it, I do. I was hurt, but I also could see I was acting so much like my father and it pissed me off. But still, I didn't change."

"Tell me about you and Abigail." Xander sat on bar stool.

"I loved her. She was the greatest love of my life. I learned to love your mother, but it wasn't a heart racing love. Abigail was the only one I ever had that with. I allowed your mother to dupe me into a marriage that I knew I shouldn't have said I would do, but it was to keep the peace with my father. Well, and to keep my inheritance. Yes, I allowed money to make my decision." John finished his Scotch and poured another.

"I was a coward for ending it by letter. Abigail knew about Elizabeth being pregnant and she knew I was being forced into the marriage, but she just let me go. I don't know if I expected her to fight for me, and for a while I was ticked that she never did, but in the end I knew it was because she loved me that she let me go. She didn't want to come between me and my family."

"Where you cheating on Abigail with Mother when she got pregnant?"

John shook his head. "Dale wasn't my child. I couldn't stand to have him in this house. He was a constant reminder of what I had to give up."

Xander drained his beer and set the bottle down. He wasn't surprised by the news, yet it still seemed to catch him off guard. His brother was only a half-brother. "Is that why I was sent away too?"

"Elizabeth said if Dale couldn't be here, you couldn't either. I'm sorry, Xander. I should have stuck up for you."

Xander stood. "We'll talk later. I need to just process all this."

"Wait. How did you find out about Abigail?"

"Grace found your letters to her."

John stared at his empty glass. "She kept them all these years." His voice dropped to a whisper, "God, Abigail, I'm so sorry."

Xander left his father to his grief. So many questions, yet a lot had been answered about his childhood. Things he never even really questioned suddenly became so clear.

He left his parents' home and headed to the McAllister barn. He didn't want to see Grace right now. He needed to wrap his mind around his father actually being in love. He never felt any love growing up between his parents, but never questioned it, since his grandparents' household was the same way. The hay loft had become his go-to place to think, albeit he usually spent his time there thinking of Grace. Today, she was on his mind, but second to the realization of how dysfunctional his family really had been.

Chapter Twenty-One

Grace sat on the couch until she could no longer hear Xander's motorcycle. In her mind, she knew by his reaction that he had no idea of the relationship between Abigail and John. But she wasn't ready to be logical quite yet. She wanted answers, and they eluded her at every turn. Bob had told her she should let it go and just concentrate on the business at hand. She had stormed out of his office and was hell bent on having it out with

Xander. Well, she had it out with him…but he hadn't fought back.

He had accused her of being insane. Maybe she was. This whole business was maddening. The mess in the basement didn't just happen. She sighed. The mess in the basement, yes, she should get that straightened out and see what else was down there.

She spent the rest of the afternoon cleaning up and repacking her mom's belongings. There was nothing else unusual down there and Grace wasted no time going through everything. Once it was straightened out, she vowed she wouldn't be back down to look again as she headed up the stairs.

Her stomach growled. A reminder that she hadn't eaten anything all day, with the exception of the cup of coffee first thing that morning. She went to the kitchen and stared out the window at the barn. *Their business*. They had to get it started, Bob reminded her this morning, or it would void the will, leaving her and Xander losing everything. Obstacles in her life at every turn. Could she not just live her life without having to please everyone else first? She was so tired of not doing what she wanted. She wanted the freedom to get on a motorcycle and just take off – like Xander. Yet, he was here with her willing to work at whatever they needed to do to get the inheritance. Would he leave her then?

Her daydreams were interrupted with the slam of the door. She asked, "Hungry?"

She turned to see Xander leaning against the kitchen door. "A little. You?"

"Starved. What do you feel like?" She wanted to apologize to Xander, yet she said nothing at first, then offered, "Let's go out for a pizza."

Xander nodded. "Give me just a few minutes to clean up. I smell like a barn."

Grace smiled as he left the room. She thought back to those kisses they shared in the hayloft. How far would it have gone had she not put the brakes on? Why was she always the practical one? She just wanted to let her hair down for once and not think of responsibility.

Grace raced upstairs with a last minute decision to put some make up on and redo her hair. She had just put on the finishing touches when a soft tap came on her door.

"It's open." She called.

Xander opened the door and smiled. "You're beautiful."

Grace stepped to him and smoothed his blue polo shirt. "You clean up pretty nice yourself."

Xander's hands rested on her hips. He gently kissed her lips. "You ready?"

Graced nodded. They rode to town in Grace's car in silence, a comfortable silence that encouraged Grace that this evening could be turned around.

They found a quiet booth in the back of the local pizza restaurant. After agreeing on a pizza and ordering, they sipped their drinks and made small talk.

"Look, Xander, I'm sorry for earlier." Grace played with the salt and pepper shakers.

"It's okay. I get where you were coming from, although you were a little crazy about it." He grinned at her.

Grace melted as she stared into his brown eyes. "Crazy? Really?" She shook her head.

Xander reached for her hand. "I went and talked to my dad after I left. I think he was a bit relieved that someone actually finally knew about it. He truly did love her. Abigail was the one great love of his life."

"But he broke it off with her?"

Xander nodded. "Yes, because he was a coward and had no backbone to stand up to my grandfather. I don't know if they had much contact after their marriages, but I would like to think that maybe living so close to each other that hopefully Dad was watching out for her."

"Did he give you any details?"

"No, not really. Let's not think about it now. Let's work on us...what we need to do to get through the next two years and then we can have our lives back."

Grace felt like she had been slapped. Xander wanted out. "Of course." She picked up her drink and took a sip.

The rest of the meal was stilted, with the only talk focusing on the horses they would be receiving to open their therapeutic riding business. Grace felt heavy hearted as they headed for home. She had hoped that Xander had wanted to see where things were going to go, yet he made it clear he wanted to move on with his life…without her.

Grace mumbled an excuse of being exhausted and headed for her room. She shut the door before she allowed the hurt to penetrate her being. The tears flowed and she slid down to the floor, leaning against the door.

Grace started when she heard a soft knock on the door. "Grace." Xander's whisper brought tears at a faster pace.

She bit her knuckle and willed herself to stop crying.

"Grace…open the door."

She stood and wiped the tears away. "What do you want, Xander? I'm tired and ready for bed."

"I don't know what I said to upset you, but I want to talk about it." Grace could feel his presence penetrating through the door.

"Not now."

"Gracie…it sounds like you've been crying. I'm coming in."

Grace scrambled to her feet and moved away from the door. She wiped her eyes and prayed that the tears would stop. She stiffened when Xander's arms came around her. She tried to pull away, yet felt her body relaxing as he pulled her back against his chest.

"Talk to me, Gracie," Xander whispered into her ear.

"It's nothing. You made it clear how you felt and you want this done with so you can move on with your life." She pushed away from him and walked to the window, looking out over the property.

"What are you talking about?"

"You said we would do what we need to do to get through the next two years and then we can have our lives back. You want your life back, I get it."

Xander chuckled. "God, woman, you totally took that wrong."

Grace turned. "You're going to stand there and laugh at me now? Please, Xander, just go."

Xander stepped over in front of her. "No. Not until we talk about this."

"There is nothing to talk about." Grace shook her head.

"I said we can have our life back...*our* meaning you and me, hopefully together."

Grace closed her eyes. It was just too much to take. It killed her to think Xander would walk out of her life for good, but it scared her just as much to think they could make a life together. "Let's not do this tonight, please. I just can't."

Xander kissed her forehead gently. "I'll see you in the morning, but we need to talk this through at some point."

Grace stood there with her eyes closed until she heard the door shut quietly. Hope. Did she dare be hopeful of a future with Xander?

Chapter Twenty-Two

Xander couldn't sleep and paced his room until four in the morning. Needing to get out of the house, he grabbed his coat and headed for the barn. The stalls needed to be readied for the arrival of the horses.

As he took inventory, his mind wandered to Grace. He didn't know how to convince her that things could work between them. Why didn't she have any faith in herself or in them? He stopped suddenly when he realized that there was a trail of straw on the floor. None had been put down yet. It was all up in the loft.

He followed the trail to the stairs to the loft. He started up them slowly. Nothing really seemed out of order, except a few bales were knocked over to the side. He glanced around and saw nothing else out of the ordinary.

He didn't give it another thought as he started to the house. A few hours had passed and he was in dire need of coffee. Xander let himself in the backdoor into the kitchen and proceeded to set up the coffee maker to start the magical brew that would kick his brain into gear.

"Why?" Grace's voice broke through the silence.

"Why what?" Xander turned to face Grace standing in the doorway, eyes blazing.

"Did you have to remove all my pictures in the living room? I know you wanted me to change things, but what…I wasn't quick enough for you?"

"What the hell are you talking about?" Xander leaned against the counter, waiting for the crazy to start flying. Lately Grace had been all over the place with her emotions.

"Don't give me that look." Grace turned and stormed from the room. Xander followed her into the living room. "Look around. What do you see?"

Xander's eyes swept over the room. At first glance not a thing was out of place. He walked around the room and looked closer. Every picture of Grace and Abigail were gone from the room. There were random pictures placed about, but nothing personal. Had Xander saw this room first, he would have assumed Grace had changed it – had made it her own.

"You think I took the pictures down?" Xander sat down on the couch and watched Grace as she paced about.

"Didn't you?"

"No. Why would I?"

Grace stopped and stared at him. "You wanted the pictures gone. You told me to make this room my own. Well, this isn't making it my own. I never would have totally depersonalized my living room."

Xander shrugged. "I don't know what to tell you. I didn't do it, Gracie."

"Stop calling me that!" Grace turned and fled up the stairs.

Xander sighed. The barn *and* the living room? Who would be moving things around if it was just him and Grace in the house? He knew it wasn't him and lately Grace seemed to have lost her marbles the way she was all over the place. Could it be that all the changes had made her a bit unstable and she just wasn't remembering things? Or was she doing it and just trying to scare Xander off?

The questions ran through his mind as he returned to the kitchen to get some coffee. It wasn't even a possibility to think about it until he had some caffeine. Pouring a cup, he looked out the window to the barn. He sipped his coffee and contemplated the changes that had been made.

He pulled out his cell phone and dialed the number of the only one that might know what was going on. He made an appointment for later in the day with Bob the lawyer. Didn't he say he had worked for her family for years? He would be the only one who could tell him if this was normal behavior for Grace under the stress of all the changes that had come to her life since the death of Abigail.

He drained his coffee and started upstairs. He turned at the top towards Grace's room. He stopped outside the door and raised his hand to knock. He paused and listened. There was no sound coming from inside the room. He shook his head and turned towards his own room. If she wanted space, she was going to get it. He wanted answers and it was obvious he wasn't going to get them from her.

Grace paced her room. Was she going insane? She knew she didn't move the pictures, yet Xander didn't seem to know anything about it. How could this be happening? Was she about to have a nervous breakdown? She flopped on her bed and stared at the ceiling. She missed her mother terribly through this – of course it was because of Abigail's wishes that she was under such stress.

It was almost too much to bear. The memories of her last year of college came flooding back to her. She had been so stressed out over school, and setting up student teaching and worrying about not graduating with honors and if she didn't, how upset her mother would be that she had almost lost her mind with a nervous breakdown. She had lost three months of school and had to postpone her student teaching. She had eventually graduated with honors and Mom had been proud of her. But the feelings were the same – feelings of inadequacy, failure and doubting herself at every turn.

She needed to find a way to reduce her stress and fast or she was going to end up in the crazy house. Just hearing that word coming from Xander almost sent her over the edge. Was she really that close to losing it all? Where were the pictures of her and Mom? Who took them? Did she?

Those months she took off from college had been filled with blackouts and blank memories. She worried now she was regressing back into the unknown. She needed to get a grip and find out how to control this stress. She couldn't afford to lose her mind. She needed to get this business venture up and running with Xander, without him questioning her mindset and whether or not she was stable. Stable was not at all what she felt at the moment.

Grace turned towards the door and hesitated. She needed to figure out what happened to the pictures that had disappeared from the living room. If she could find them, she might be able to figure why Xander took them. She opened the door with renewed determination. As she started down the stairs, she heard the roar of Xander's motorcycle leaving the driveway. Fine, let him leave for the day. It would give her the peace and quiet she needed.

Chapter Twenty-Three

Xander pulled up in front of the lawyer's office. Bob had been very vague on the phone, but Xander hoped with a face to face conversation, Bob would be more forthcoming with any information he needed. He sighed as he started for the door. He had a feeling this wasn't going to be easy.

Xander sat in a chair in the waiting room. Bob's secretary had been very clear it would be a little bit before he was available. Xander wondered if this was a ploy to avoid this whole conversation.

"Sebastian, what can I do for you?" Bob held out his hand in greeting.

Shaking the lawyer's hand, Xander made a split second decision to play along with the coy comment. "Well, just some quick questions about some history that might help us with what is going on in the house?"

"What kind of history?" Bob moved around his desk and sat down, gesturing for Xander to take a seat.

"Well, any paranormal activity, any other issues with Grace, such as mental instability?" Xander smiled, keeping the mood light.

"What? No, of course not to either. Why would you ask that?"

Xander crossed his legs. "Well, there seems to be some things that have just up and moved themselves."

"What kind of things?" Bob sat forward.

"Straw bales tripped over, some pictures taken from the living room, and the basement had been tossed." Xander studied Bob's face carefully.

No expression, too neutral. "What would you know about that?"

"Not a thing. Sounds like a practical joke." Bob leaned back in his chair and kept eye contact with Xander.

"Come on, really? A practical joke? Grace doesn't seem like the type to do pranks, and she was too upset with the pictures gone this morning."

"I don't know. Was there something specific you thought I could tell you?"

Xander sighed in frustration. "What is going on with Grace? I know she showed up here to talk to you about Abigail's letters and now things are just weird."

"Look, there is nothing that is being hidden from you, if that is what you are thinking. She did ask about the letters and I'm sure she told you it was your father who wrote them. Other than that, Grace has had a pretty much normal life with the typical issues between mom and daughter that most girls have." He paused and cleared his throat. "She had a bit of a tough time in college, but it was nothing but stress and she's none the worse for it."

"What kind of tough time?"

"That's something that you would have to ask her." Bob stood to indicate their meeting was over. "How are things going between you two, anyway?"

Xander stood and shook Bob's hand. "Fine." The lie unsettled Xander. He didn't want to admit it, but this was going to be a huge obstacle to overcome.

He left the room more frustrated than when he arrived. Something was going on and he wanted to know what it was. Once on his motorcycle, he turned towards the coast – the ride he had taken Grace on the first time she rode his bike with him. He lost himself to the hum of the motor. As he became one with the bike, his mind drifted to the time since he had reconnected with Grace. How he longed for the time when they first met and were getting to know each other – before she realized he was a Stevens. He would do anything to change where he came from.

He pulled off the road and stared down at the ocean. The waves mesmerized him and he let each wave mentally wash over him and take away the stress. He smiled at the memory of Grace's eyes lighting up at the sight here. Her features had softened and she had immediately let down her guard, as brief as that had been.

This was where they needed to come to talk. The sound of the waves, the sight of the blue-green lapping at the sand below, was the perfect spot for both of them to relax and let their guards down and really talk to each other. With renewed determination, Xander turned the bike towards home – funny he was thinking of it as home – and the excitement to see Grace once again overtook him.

Chapter Twenty-Four

Grace wandered around the living room, opening every drawer and cabinet. Still not finding the pictures, she moved on to the foyer and the closet. She searched through the jackets, the boxes on the shelf—nothing. She shut the door with a bit more force than she intended and groaned. Where could they be? Where would Xander have put them?

She paced around the foyer and stopped in front of the stairs before continuing to pace. She stopped two more times in between pacing at the stairs. Would he have put them in his room? She started up the stairs and stopped halfway. Could she go through his room before he got back? Did she really want to?

She had wanted to believe that Xander was different from other guys. He had seemed pretended to be so open and honest. She shook her head. There was no other explanation. Xander had to be the one who moved the pictures. Squaring her shoulders, she took the stairs two at a time and ran down the hallway to Xander's door. It was shut and she hesitated before turning the knob.

She glanced around. It was a lot cleaner than she expected. Not a thing out of place, clothes hung up neatly in the closet. The closet door was open, but everything was neat and orderly. She stepped inside and listened. Still no sound of the motorcycle coming back. She gave a little prayer that she would hear it. She definitely didn't want to Xander catching her in his room. She tiptoed to the end of his bed. She giggled at herself, trying to be so quiet when no one was there to hear her.

She laid a hand on the blanket folded at the foot of the bed and closed her eyes. She had fallen for Xander, fallen harder for him than she had ever done before. She shook her head and backed out of the room. She couldn't do it. She wanted to believe in him, to trust him and this would only cause problems, even if he never found out. She turned towards her room as she heard the motorcycle coming up the driveway. Whew! She finally made a good decision.

"Grace!" Xander's voice broke through her thoughts as the front door slammed shut.

She moved to the top of the stairs. "I'm right here."

She looked down as he approached the bottom of the stairs and looked up at her. His hair was messed up from his helmet. His cheeks were flushed and her heart skipped a beat.

"Let's pack a picnic and take a ride up the coast. We can enjoy the sunset over the ocean."

"Seriously? Just yesterday you were calling me insane and now you want me to go out with you?"

Xander ran his fingers through his hair. "Look, we need to talk and I think we could do a lot better if we were out of this house." He turned away and then turned back. "Please, Gracie…"

She stared down the stairs at him. He looked like a lost soul just standing there, his eyes pleading with her to say yes. "Fine."

Her heart beat faster as a smile lit up his face. "Great. I'll pack up something for us. Bring a sweatshirt. It will be cold on the way back."

She nodded, but realized he had already turned towards the kitchen. She shook her head as she turned towards her room to change.

She tugged on a pair of jeans and t-shirt. Yanking open her closet door, she reached up to the shelf to grab a sweatshirt. Her fingers brushed something hard. *What is that?* Grabbing her small step stool, she stood upon it to see the shelf. Pushed back, under her sweatshirt, was a stack of framed pictures. As she pulled out the top one, she gasped realizing they were the pictures from the living room that had disappeared. *Had she put them here? No, she couldn't be having blackouts again.*

She pushed the frame back onto the shelf. Grabbing her sweatshirt, she closed her closet door. She frantically tried to figure out how she would have taken the pictures and had no recollection. Even when she was having the black outs, she hadn't taken things. Mostly just showed up at places that she had no memory of. Berating herself for allowing the stress to get to her, she vowed to make a doctor's appointment and get to the bottom of this. But tonight, she was going to just enjoy Xander's company – away from the house and the inheritance and any ill feelings she might have at the moment. She wanted to just let go and enjoy the night for what it was.

Neither spoke while Xander filled his saddle bags with the food he had packed. The silence continued while Grace put on a helmet and settled behind him. Once the motorcycle was running,

Xander patted her leg and ran his hand slowly down her calf before starting down the driveway. Grace knew it was his way of reassuring her, knowing the motorcycle made her a bit nervous and she was grateful for his kindness. Every time she wanted to think negative of him, he would do something like this – something generous and sincere that made her question her own doubts of him.

Grace found herself relaxing as she leaned against Xander's back and held on loosely. She closed her eyes and just enjoyed the hum of the bike and the feel of his hard muscles moving as he controlled the bike. She sighed softly and allowed herself to give into the "what if's" running through her mind. What if Xander chose to stay after the two year period? What if Xander fell in love with her like she was starting to do?

She opened her eyes and took in the scenery. Xander had turned onto a side road that Grace had never gone down before. It curved around the coast and out onto a peninsula where a lighthouse came into view.

As Xander shut off the bike and the sound quieted, the waves crashing on the rocks surrounding them washed over Grace. Her lips turned up in a soft smile as she closed her eyes and just listened.

"Ready?" Xander's soft voice broke her daydreaming.

Grace got off the bike and waited for Xander to grab the food. She took in the area around her – secluded and breathtaking. The lighthouse was a small one and looked to be privately maintained. She took a few steps towards it and stopped, glancing back.

"Go ahead and explore." Xander chuckled.

Grace didn't need to be told twice. She circled around the lighthouse on the grassy area and stopped at the end. Jagged rocks spread below her and the white foam from the waves sprayed up to greet her. She breathed in the salty air and peace settled about her shoulders, wiping away the stress from the past few days.

"It's gorgeous, isn't it?"

"What is this place? I have never even seen a sign for a lighthouse in this area." Grace turned to face him.

"It's a privately owned one. I haven't been here in years and really only just remembered about it earlier today. I thought you would like it."

Grace watched Xander spread out a blanket and put the bag of food at the corner. He pulled out a bottle of wine and proceeded to uncork it. She sat down on the blanket and faced the water. The sounds soothed her anxious nerves.

"Grace." Xander's soft whisper broke through her thoughts. She glanced over and took the glass of wine he offered her. Sipping it, her mind raced with what to think. Xander was once again the man she had started to fall in love with – the one before the inheritance disaster. She had to stay sharp and not let her guard down.

"So what is it you wanted to talk about?" She kept her eyes averted from him. To drink in the chocolate of his eyes would be the final blow to the wall she had carefully erected around her heart. She fought hard to deny the feelings she felt for Xander.

"I just wanted to get away from the house, talk about something other than the business plan or what we had to do for you to get the inheritance." Xander leaned back on one elbow while he took a drink from his glass of wine.

"Me to get the inheritance? I thought this was both of us." Grace glanced over to him.

"I don't want it, Gracie. I'd rather spend time with you, just you and I, the way it was after the funeral when we were getting to know each other." He sat up. His fingers touched her chin, directing her to look at him. "I want you back, the you that was so excited to do something different, to live her life the way she never thought she could."

"It seemed so easy just a few weeks ago, didn't it?" Grace searched his eyes. Sadness filled her, but there was hope...a hope for the two of them. She sat mesmerized as his face came closer to her, his lips hovering just short of touching hers. "Xander?"

"Shhh, Grace, don't think. Let's just have this moment." His voice got softer with each word as he came closer, the last word really just a breath on her lips before he closed the gap and claimed her mouth with his.

The kiss was gentle, yet demanding. Grace reached to the side to put down the glass, not even caring if it tipped over. Once her hand was free, she reached for the back of his neck and ran her fingers through the edges of his hair. He pushed her back onto the blanket, deepening the kiss as she let out a soft moan.

Apparently encouraged by her receptiveness, Xander ran his hand along her side, pushing up her t-shirt as he slowly caressed her skin. Her breathing became heavy as she moved against him, wanting no distance between them. She pulled him closer, and he settled between her legs. He broke off the kiss, looking down at her.

"Grace, I want you..."

She nodded and smiled. "I want you too, Xander." The sounds of the waves crashed against the rocks and she closed her eyes. "But now probably isn't the best time or place."

"It's private here. No one will find us." Xander tried to rein in his thoughts, but it was so hard to think with the raging hard on pushing against his zipper.

A lone tear escaped Grace's eye. Xander brushed it away with his thumb. "What is it?"

She shook her head. She had to control her thoughts, her feelings for this man. This could be all part of the manipulation. Use her, screw her and then take what he wants. She tried to stop the negative thoughts from bombarding her, but they seemed out of control.

She pushed him off her and stood, yanking down her shirt. "I think we should go."

"Grace…what happened?" Xander took a deep breath and closed his eyes while he exhaled.

"Just take me home." Grace picked up the glass that had tipped over and threw it into the bag. She walked to the edge of the rocks and stared down at the water. Could she walk away from it all?

Including the inheritance, which would allow her to walk away from Xander? She couldn't stand the feelings of uneasiness that hit her every time he was around. The wanting for more, and then the fear he was using her.

She startled at the roar of the motorcycle. She turned and Xander had packed everything away and was waiting for her. She mouthed "I'm sorry" to him as she walked towards the bike. He gave her a stiff nod and waited until she got seated and held on before he took off.

Grace cried all the way home, tears drying to her face from the wind blowing. She wanted nothing more than to bury herself into Xander's back and beg him to forgive her. As they turned into the driveway, Grace looked up at the house as it came into sight. This was the house that was going to destroy any chance of happiness she had.

They both were silent as they entered the house. Grace turned toward Xander and he just shook his head and headed to the kitchen. "Xander, wait."

He stopped and turned slowly to face her. "What?"

"I'm sorry. I just can't help if this is all part of your plan."

Xander tossed the bag onto a nearby chair and strode to her until he was looking down at her. His hands rested on her hips as he pulled her close. "I want you, Grace. It has nothing to do with the damn house or anything else. Damn it, why can't you just trust that this is what I am feeling?" He pulled her hard against him and kissed her, his tongue opening her mouth and stroking hers.

She leaned against him and allowed the onslaught of the demanding kiss from him, wanting to allow herself to surrender to the passion. He broke off the kiss. "If you can't feel my love for you, I don't know how else to show you."

"Love?"

Xander took a step back. He slowed his breathing and watched her. "Yes, Grace. Somewhere, somehow I fell in love with you. I didn't plan on it, but it happened. Damn it, woman, you are infuriating. I'm not out to get you."

"You lied to me about who you were! How am I supposed to just trust everything you say now?"

"I didn't lie really." Xander ran his fingers through his hair. He turned and paced the foyer. "I didn't know how to tell you. And I certainly didn't plan on falling in love with you."

"You didn't know about your father and Mom?" Grace's accusing tone stopped Xander in his pacing.

"No, I didn't. How many times do I have to tell you that?"

Grace shook her head. "I don't know what to believe." She let out a sob and ran for the stairs.

"Grace, don't go. Let's talk about this."

She shook her head as she fled to her room. She couldn't bear to hear him tell her he loved her while she fought that love with everything she had inside her.

Chapter Twenty-Five

Grace spent the night tossing and turning, sleep eluding her. She sat up and glanced at the clock. Three A.M. She sighed as she pushed the covers back and swung her legs over the side of the bed. She sat there and stared out the window at the moon. She wanted to go to Xander and finish what had been started at the lighthouse.

She opened her door slowly, listening for any little sound that would indicate that Xander was awake. Of course he would be asleep at this hour.

She crept down the hallway and listened again. She stopped at the end of the hall, in front of his bedroom door. The window at the end of the hallway looked out on the back of the house.

She leaned against the cool pane and took a deep breath. She wanted him, she couldn't deny that. Out of the corner of her eye, she saw a glow outside. Squinting to get a better look, registration dawned on her that the barn was on fire. She turned and pounded on Xander's door.

"Xander, get up!" Grace opened the door, still pounding on it as it swung open.

"Grace, what's the matter?" Xander lifted his head.

"The barn... fire." Grace pointed out the window.

"Call the fire department." Xander jumped out of bed and reached for his pants.

Grace briefly registered the moonlight bouncing of his bare abs before she ran for the stairs to make the call. She was on the phone in the kitchen when Xander ran past her, headed for the barn. Thankfully the horses weren't scheduled to arrive until the next day. Grace swallowed hard and wondered how this would affect their business.

She followed Xander outside, where sirens could be heard. Xander had the hose out and was spraying what he could, but the fire engulfed the barn. It was obvious to see the building would be a total loss. All that hard work that Mom had done to build this and arrange everything for her and Xander to be together to carry out her dreams—it was gone in an instant.

Grace choked back the tears as the firefighters pulled Xander away from the building. They kept the water on it, but mainly to contain it from spreading any further. She looked up through her tears as Xander walked towards her. He folded her into his arms and held her close to his chest.

"It's going to be okay." He whispered into her hair.

She nodded and held him close. "What are we going to do?"

"Not a thing tonight. It's just about out. Why don't we go make some coffee?" Xander pulled her to his side, his arm never leaving her waist. and walked her slowly back to the house.

"It's all gone. All of Mom's dreams." Grace muttered in disbelief, shaking her head.

"We'll work it out. We can rebuild." Xander soothed her, his arm holding her close.

Grace sat on a barstool as Xander started the coffee maker. He had offered coffee to the fire department and knew there would be a few pots made tonight. He put together a thermos and started another pot.

"I'm going to run this out to the guys out there. Stay right here, Gracie."

She nodded as he headed out the door. Her mind reeled with new complications to this arrangement they had to tackle. Now they had to start from scratch just as things were falling into place. Well, not everything had fallen into place. She glanced at the clock just as Xander walked back into the kitchen.

Five o'clock. "Is it too early to call Bob? He needs to know what is going on." Grace spoke out loud, although it was more to herself.

"Probably still a little early." Xander placed a cup of coffee in front of her. He reached for her hand. "It will be okay."

Grace gripped his hand. She just wanted to pull strength from him. He was a rock and she felt ready to dissolve into a million pieces.

"How did you see the fire?" Xander leaned against the counter, watching Grace carefully.

"What?" Grace looked up, confused. "Oh, the fire. I was, I couldn't sleep."

Xander nodded. "You couldn't sleep and…where did you see it from, Grace?"

"I was in the hallway. I…I…" Her voice trailed off as she looked into his eyes. *She couldn't tell him she was going to him.* Grace shook her head. "It doesn't matter."

"You've got to talk to me. What is going on?" Xander started another pot of coffee and turned back towards Grace. "Please, Gracie, talk to me."

"There's nothing to say. Whatever progress we had made towards this manipulation of Mom, it's gone. All gone."

Xander came around the island and pulled her into his arms. "It doesn't matter. Damn it, I don't care about that. We can rebuild. I want to know what is really on your mind."

Grace shook her head. "We just need to stick to the plan and get this business up and running." Grace made the mistake of looking up into his eyes. "Xander, we can't do this."

He kissed her gently. "Do what? Love each other?"

"I don't know how I'm feeling." Grace pushed away to put some distance between them.

"I know you want me. I can see it every time I look into your eyes. I feel it in your kisses." Xander took a step back. "But you take all the time you need. I'm not going anywhere."

Grace nodded before turning towards the window. Watching the firemen keep the blaze under control, Grace shook her head. "How do you think the fire started?"

"I don't know. Guess the fire chief will let us know when they've had time to investigate."

"What now?" Grace turned towards him. "Where do we go from here with Mom's restrictions?"

Xander sighed. "I don't have any answers, Gracie. We'll have to talk to Bob in the morning, in a few hours. Why don't you try and get some sleep?"

Grace left the kitchen. There had never been anything so drastically done when she had previous blackouts. Could she have sabotaged this business unconsciously to rebel against Mom's manipulation? She didn't want the business. Hell, at this point, she didn't even want the house. She wanted her normal, quiet life back – the life before Xander, the life where she didn't feel the urge to become alive. The one where she knew what was expected of her and she could just accept that. Instead, every time she looked into a mirror, she saw a young woman looking for excitement and love, the same thing she felt every time she looked at Xander.

In her heart she knew he wasn't really the enemy. But could she trust him?

Chapter Twenty-Six

Xander stared at the empty coffee mug. He had been sitting here all night trying to find the answers that Grace wanted. He had no idea how he was going to undo all the damage that seemed to have been done last night. The fire was a separate issue. All he knew was that he wanted his life back. He didn't give a damn about the business or the inheritance, not if Grace was that unhappy. He wanted to see the sparkle in her eyes again, see her smile when she tried a new adventure and through it all he wanted to be by her side.

He sighed as he put his mug in the sink. The barn was nothing but a pile of embers and the firefighters doused it one more time with water to kill those too. The barn had been a total loss. No idea where it had started, but one thing was for sure, it was a major setback in the time frame they had to get the horses and get the business up and running. Xander cursed under his breath. He glanced at the clock. Seven a.m. Still too early to make any phone calls.

He grabbed his motorcycle keys and headed for the door. He couldn't ignore the pit in his stomach screaming at him that this was all wrong. Grace's brokenness last night was like a sucker punch to the gut. He stopped briefly in the foyer to scribble a note to Grace to let her know he had gone into town and would be back later. He hoped she fell back asleep.

He turned his bike towards town. He maintained a slow pace, trying to kill time. Arriving at *Daisy's*, he went in and ordered a cinnamon roll and a coffee. He sat at a table watching the town start to come awake with a few stragglers walking towards their work. One or two people popped into the coffee shop and left. Xander basically was left alone with his thoughts. He processed what he thought he wanted in life, but it all came back to Grace. When did he fall head over heels in love with her? And when did he suddenly want to settle down and have a family?

He drained his cup of coffee and threw his trash out. Turning towards the lawyer's office, he prayed that Bob was one that arrived early for work. Xander needed answers to bring to Grace. He was greeted by a locked door and no signs of life around the office. Xander shook his head and grumbled. Didn't anyone work these days at eight a.m.? He glanced at his watch and realized it wasn't even eight yet.

He turned towards the rest of Main Street and decided to do some window shopping, praying

Bob would arrive soon. He came upon the florist putting buckets of flowers outside her door.

"Are you open?"

"I can be. Need something special?"

Xander smiled. "Can you mix me a dozen of red and yellow roses?"

"Absolutely. Come on in."

Xander wandered around the store while the shop owner gathered the two colors of roses and made a beautiful bouquet of them.

"You're all set."

Xander paid her and after having her put them in a box so they would be easier to carry on the motorcycle, he turned and headed for his bike. Forget Bob right now. He just wanted to see Grace and talk with her. They had come to an understanding. Damn it, he knew the way she felt about him even if she didn't yet.

Xander's ride back was much quicker than the ride to town had been. He grabbed the box of flowers and ran up the front stairs. As he ran in the house, he stopped short at the sound of voices in the living room.

"What are our options?" Grace's voice trembled and Xander could picture her lacing her fingers together in what he learned to be her nervous habit.

Bob's voice broke through Xander's thoughts. "There are options, Grace. Don't you worry."

Xander laid the box on the table and strode into the living room. Bob stood and extended his hand. Xander gripped his hand in a firm shake. "I had gone to town to talk to you."

"Grace called me at home first thing this morning." Bob sat back down. "I'm glad she did."

"I didn't know you had gone to see Bob…your note didn't specify."

Xander nodded as he sat down next to her. He reached for her and covered her clasped hands with his. "I was rather hoping to talk to you after Grace and I had a chance to talk things through. I…"

Grace pulled her hands from Xander's and turned to face him. "What do you mean? We need to know what to do with this business. You remember there is a time crunch here...we have to run this thing for two years and I know how much you want to be done with it all."

Xander glanced at Bob and sighed. "I don't want to be done with it all. I don't want to be restricted in my life by Abigail's wishes. Damn it, Grace. We need to talk about this."

"What's to talk about? We have no choice but to get the business up and going." Grace pushed off the couch and paced in front of the fireplace. "I know what you're going to say so don't. I can't even think about that right now."

Bob stood. "I think you two need to talk this through. If, and when, you decide to move forward with the business, I'll be around to help you with the necessary paperwork. But remember, there is a time crunch, but that doesn't mean you have to go through with it." He shook Xander's hand and turned towards Grace. He pulled her into a hug.

"Grace, use your heart when you think about this decision. Abigail's intent was never for you to be unhappy."

Grace kissed his cheek and nodded. She watched Bob walk out before closing her eyes. She took a deep breath and exhaled slowly. She turned to face Xander and held her hand up for him not to speak. "Why are you doing this? Do you want me to lose everything?"

"Of course not. I want you to be happy." Xander took a step towards her. "You were the one that said you never wanted this. You wanted to teach your 'kids' and not be stuck in this place. Your words." He sighed. "Grace, I want to see that smile when you try something new. You never smile anymore."

Grace shook her head. "I know that is what I said, but this is all I have left of my family. Don't you get that?" She turned to leave the room, turning back at the doorway. "Don't you dare try to take that away from me."

Xander plopped down on the couch. How did that backfire on him? He wanted so badly just for her to be happy, to go back to that moment when he was getting to know her.

Chapter Twenty-Seven

Grace's hands tingled. She clenched a fist and released, then repeated again and again to try and release the stress building up in her. She had no idea what she had been doing. Everything in the past couple of weeks was a blur and now Xander wanted out. She knew he wasn't the type to settle down. He said it, but he wanted out of the inheritance, which would make it easier for him to run. Alone. That is what she would be if he left.

That simple word left her feeling cold inside—cold and scared to death.

She pulled open her closet door and reached for the pile of pictures up on the shelf. She sat down on her bed with the pictures and slowly perused them. Pictures of her mom and dad, pictures of her as a child, her and her mom, her with her dad. All of them happy, smiling. Grace wiped away a tear as it rolled down her cheek. She had a good childhood and suddenly everything was ripped apart. Her mom had been in love with Xander's dad before her dad came into the picture. Would Grace even be alive had her mom been with John and stayed with him?

Her whole life seemed like a lie at this moment. She pulled the last picture of her and her mom close to her chest as she lay back on the bed and cried. Tears washed away the anger directed at Xander and left her feeling empty. What did she want out of life? Did she want to continue to live here in her childhood home? Not really, but she had been looking forward to starting the therapeutic riding center for sensory needs kids with the hope that after the business got up and running that she could go back to teaching her beloved second grade.

Grace didn't know how much time had passed when she finally stood up and put the pictures away. She must have drifted off and slept a bit. Her stomach gnawed at her as hunger took over. She pulled open the door and there was a box outside her door. She reached down, pulling off the cover. Inside she found a dozen yellow and red roses mixed with baby's breath, the scent bombarding her as she inhaled deeply.

A small card tucked in the side caught her eye. She pulled it out and read.

I simply love you.

Tears welled up in her eyes again. Xander. Only he would do this and cut straight to the heart of things. She had been fighting hard to keep him at arm's length, but her heart screamed at her to just let him love her and for her to love him in return. She needed to tell him about the blackouts.

She heard a curse from downstairs and picked up the box to hurry down to the kitchen. She stopped short as she saw Xander wandering from cupboard to cupboard, slamming doors.

"What are you doing?" Grace stepped to the bar and put down the flowers. "Thank you by the way."

Xander turned. "You're welcome." He paused and leaned against the counter. "Since you don't cook, you want to tell me why you rearranged everything?"

Grace looked around in confusion. "What are you talking about?"

Xander opened a couple of the cupboard doors and pointed. "Look. Nothing is the same. Are you trying to get me to leave? Because that won't do it, Although I will say, I will put it all back the way I find it easiest, since I'm cooking."

Grace went to the cupboard over the refrigerator to get a vase. They weren't there. "I didn't do this."

Xander snorted. "Who did then? The ghost that apparently is living in this house."

"Don't be like that...I didn't...I don't think..." Grace trailed off. Did she do this? When would she have done it? Grace busied herself with preparing the roses to go in water. She glanced up when Xander placed a vase in front of her.

"Look, I don't want to fight. I want to figure this out so you're happy." Xander reached for her hand and entwined his fingers with hers. "Don't you realize that? It's always been about your happiness."

Grace nodded. "I don't know how to..." She closed her eyes and took a deep breath. "I'm afraid to let you in, Xander. Nothing good ever comes from me allowing someone in my heart."

"I get you've been hurt. We both have, but I promise it's worth the risk of loving." Xander raised her hand to his lips and kissed it softly. "Just think about it."

Grace stood there staring at the roses as Xander left the room. She raised a yellow and a red bloom to her nose and inhaled. How did he know that these two colors mixed together were her ultimate favorite? At the thought of it, her heart melted just a bit more. She finished arranging the flowers, allowing her thoughts to drift to Xander and the what if's.

She caught a glimpse of people around the barn. She started for the remaining ashes hoping to get some answers from the fire chief. She stopped short as she got closer. Conflict ran through her, making her stomach clench in fear. They had been so close to getting the business that her mom had wanted up and running and now it was over. Defeat dragged her shoulders down. She needed to give up on this. They would lose her family's house, but was Xander right – that love could be worth the risk? She had never felt this way about anyone before, not even when she thought she was in love.

Xander consumed her every thought. She would find herself smiling during the day just at the thought of him. She knew deep down in her gut she couldn't walk away from him. A sigh of resignation escaped her. The real question was, should she give up following her mother's wishes just so she could be happy? When did it become about her and not trying to please everyone else, even in death?

Grace approached the firemen working around the barn, making sure embers were watered down. "Is the chief here?"

A young firefighter glanced up. "No, ma'am. He went back to town to finish up some paperwork. He mentioned coming back later to talk to you."

Grace nodded. "Thanks." She turned back towards the house. The waiting game never ended. Waiting on the fire chief, waiting on the time lapse to do Abigail's wishes, waiting on...on herself to make a decision about what needed to be done.

She pondered her options back to the house. She stepped into the kitchen and her eyes came to rest on the roses Xander had given her. The icy walls around her heart melted just a little bit more every time she looked at them. What was she afraid of? Yes, it was true she had been hurt in the past, but nothing that she couldn't bounce back from. It was more the way Xander made her feel that scared her. The feeling that she could do anything she put her mind to. She was more afraid of success than she was failure. Maybe that was why it was easy to think about throwing in the towel on the therapeutic riding lessons that they had planned. It would be just another failure if they gave up on it, and Grace was used to that feeling.

Success, on the other hand, scared her. What if she did make it? And was really successful? It would change her life forever, and others' too, if the success was done right. Could she allow herself to be happy and to wonder what would happen if she allowed success to happen? Was she sabotaging her happiness?

Chapter Twenty-Eight

Xander walked through the woods, listening to the birds and trying to find his center again. Grace had him off balance and not thinking straight. If only his father hadn't been involved with Abigail, then there wouldn't be so much distrust from Grace. Or would there? Xander came to a large boulder under a canopy of trees. Shaded and cool, he climbed on the rock and lay back.

He needed to reach Grace somehow. He didn't care about the inheritance, but he didn't want her to lose it if that is what she truly wanted. But somehow, someway he needed to reach her and let her know how much he had fallen in love with her. Her smile, her infectious laughter when she tried something new, the excitement overriding the fear in her eyes at new adventures, and most of all the banter the two of them had. She could bring him to tears with laughter at her wit and amazing sense of humor.

She could pull no punches when they were at ease with each other telling him exactly what she thought, being open and honest about always feeling that she had to do the right thing, yet she shared with him her hopes and dreams, ones he knew she had never shared before. He would court her if he had to, as old fashion as that sounded, he would win her heart over with flowers and poetry, with being sincere and showing her how much she truly meant and what an amazing woman she was, despite the way she felt as an outsider in her own home.

Love would become infectious and he could only hope it would be allowed to bloom between them before they were torn apart by this ridiculous plan of Abigail's. There had to be more to it. In all the years he had known Abigail, he never would have imagined her pulling off something so cruel and rigid that could ensure her daughter lose everything.

With renewed hope in his heart, Xander started back to the house. He would give Grace her space, at least for the moment, until a plan formed for his wooing her. He would make her see how truly incredible she was.

The following few days passed quickly with meetings with Bob and what needed to be done to rebuild the barn. They were able to postpone the arrival of the horses. Although Grace and Xander kept a distance from each other and didn't talk other than about the project, Xander had hope that even when they talked, that Grace would be open to him. He had been wracking his brain on how to reach her when the idea came to him.

"I'm headed out for the day, Grace. Do you need anything?" Xander leaned against the doorframe of her bedroom.

Grace glanced up and shook her head no before looking back down at the book she was reading.

Xander sighed. "I'll be back later than."

Grace simply nodded. She waited until she heard the door shut before she put the book down. It had been a tough few days, keeping Xander at arm's length when she wanted to melt against him and just let him fight all the problems for her. She wanted to give up and run away with him, in hopes of getting back to the way they had been when they were first getting to know each other.

She had made the tough choice to put the wall up and leave it. The roses had been a nice touch and almost had her, but she couldn't fold into the romanticism that Xander seemed to be bringing on. She needed to get through the next couple of years and she was determined that she would let her guard down only after they had achieved Mom's dream.

Xander had certainly stepped up the past few days, taking on all the phones calls and responsibility of arranging for the barn to be rebuilt. A crew was out there working now. The hammering and saws cutting through the quietness were a constant reminder of the setback they suffered.

The Chief reported slight clues of a possible arson, but it wasn't cut and dry and the fire marshall was hesitant to label it as such. Grace was afraid it would soon be a thing of the past, unsolved and they would never know. In her gut, she knew that someone was behind it and for once she was relieved to know for sure it wasn't her and a blackout moment. The frustration level was something she was learning to deal with, but she longed for simpler days when her mom was alive and they could just sit and talk. The irony was not lost on her that she wouldn't be in this predicament if her mother still lived.

The ringing doorbell brought Grace out of her daydreaming. As she reached the door, she took a deep breath before opening it. They didn't have many visitors here. She couldn't imagine who would be on the other side. She swung open the door to come face to face with John Stevens.

"Grace."

"Xander's not here." Grace's tone chilled the air between them.

"Well, good. I'm not here to see Sebastian, but you instead." John offered a tentative smile.

Grace paused. Spurred by her upbringing, she stepped back and gestured for John to step into the house. As she closed the door behind him, she tried to clear her mind, as it was a whirlwind of possibilities of what he could possibly want to talk to her about. Did he want to offer her a way out of this mess? Insist that she stay out of Xander's life?

"Grace?" His soft voice broke through her thoughts.

"Excuse my manners. Please, right this way." She led the way to the living room. She perched on the end of the couch and waited until John had settled into the easy chair.

John cleared his throat. "I don't know really where to start. I'm here because…"

Grace waited. "I'm not going anywhere, Mr. Stevens. This was my mother's house and I intend to keep it in the family."

John's eyes widened. "You think I want you to leave? Of course not."

"Well, what could you possibly want? I can't imagine this was an easy place for you to visit, it being beneath you and all."

John shook his head. "Grace, I know I have that reputation, but please let me explain. No, this isn't easy for me, but not for the reasons you are insinuating."

Grace sat back on the couch. She kept her guard up, although she was intrigued as to what Xander's dad could possibly want here.

"I don't know even where to start. Grace, I know you found the letters from me to your mom."

Grace nodded and waited for him to continue.

"I loved Abigail. She was the one person who I could be myself with and I blew it."

Grace closed her eyes and tried to picture her mom with John. "I don't understand why you are here, Mr. Stevens."

"John, please. I know this probably is out of the blue, but I need to explain."

Grace nodded. "Okay, go ahead."

John stood and paced the room. "Abigail was the love of my life and we really had something, but I allowed my father to stop it. I was not strong, not like Sebastian, Xander." He paused and faced her. "Abigail and I had the chance to talk after your dad died. And she forgave me, Grace. I want you to forgive me, too."

"You don't need my forgiveness."

John sat down on the edge of the couch next to Grace. "I do. Grace, I want this to stop, this feuding between families. I see the way Sebastian, Xander, lights up when he says your name. He loves you and you are good for him. I have never seen my son want to put down roots and actually be involved in anything. You bring out the best in him, you make him a better man."

"Mr. Stevens, we were thrown into this by Abigail. Xander and I didn't have a choice." Grace clenched her hands together. "I don't understand why she would do this."

John covered Grace's hands with his hand and patted hers gently. "Grace, Abigail knew how it tore me apart not to be a part of my son's life. I listened to my wife and sent him away. It killed me every day not having contact with him."

"Why then?"

John sighed. "What I'm about to tell you is in no way a reflection on your mom. Abigail was a saint and she didn't deserve what I did to her."

"I know you got Mrs. Stevens pregnant while you were dating Mom."

John shook his head. "No. Elizabeth said I got her pregnant and I went along with my father's wishes to marry her so there wouldn't be a scandal. Dale is not my child."

"Then why? Why did you allow Abigail to believe that?"

"Because I was a coward and I didn't know what else to do. She didn't deserve the way I left things and she certainly didn't deserve the way my father treated her. Your mother had more refinement and dignity than anyone I have ever known."

"I don't understand. Why are you telling me this?"

John thought for a moment. "Because I want you to understand what a fool I was and how sorry I am. Abigail and I became friends again after your Dad died. She kept me informed of what Sebastian was up to and she gave him what I couldn't."

"Your wife must have been furious."

"She didn't know. And I'm not saying that was the right thing to do, but let's be honest. Elizabeth is a snob and quite frankly a bitch. She was the perfect one for the family according to my father, God rest his soul, but he was wrong. I played along with the charade because I was an idiot and didn't have the courage to stand up to my father. I was wrong, Grace, so wrong, and I wish I could turn back the time and change it all."

Grace nodded. She got it, but she didn't. It brought more questions than answers and she didn't want to think about it.

"I just still don't understand why you think I need to know this." Grace held her breath. Did Xander put him up to coming here.

"I can see it in your eyes. No, Sebastian doesn't know I'm here." John sat back. "I'm here because you need to know I'm thrilled Sebastian has you in his life and he would never want my 'blessing' because we are so far apart right now. Something I hope to change someday. But, Grace, he loves you and you are the best thing that has happened to him. It's time for this feud to end between our families. It has gone on long enough. Don't let it ruin another generation of love."

John stood and started to the door. Grace stared after him and stood as he turned back towards her. "Just think about it, please." He gave her a smile and left. Grace sank back into the couch. Her mind was filled with the possibilities. Did Xander truly love her? He said he did...the card with the flowers declared it...but did she trust her instinct enough to let him in?

She wanted to. She longed for that kind of love that was shown in her mom's letters from John. She wanted that in her life, but she turned cold at the thought of being hurt. The thought that it might not last due to stupidness within the families and the past feud. Did she dare open up just a little to take the risk?

Chapter Twenty-Nine

Xander sat at the lighthouse. His thoughts drifted to the last time he was here with Grace. He closed his eyes and allowed the sound of the crashing waves to wash over him. As he found his balance, he withdrew his pad of paper and pen, opened his eyes and began to write.

He had been drifting for so long through his adult life, he almost forgot what it was like to feel a calmness through him as he settled into nature and just allow it to balance out the stress. Through the years he had found himself moving from job to job, place to place, but always kept in an area that he could easily be near the ocean or near a wooden area to keep that balance in his life that only nature could bring him. Since this whole situation had started with Grace, he had forgotten how much he needed this.

This was a part of himself he wanted to share with Grace for the first time in his adult life, he wanted to share himself with another person. She had moved right into his heart and she didn't even know it. He wanted her to know him, the real him, the him that he hid from so many people in an effort to stay under the radar. There had been enough people in the limelight with his parents. He was so jaded from the social classes and being one of them that he did everything he could to do quite the opposite of what was expected of him. Yet Grace had no expectations of him. She simply brought out the best in him without trying. He exhaled and allowed the words to flow through his pen and onto the paper, words that would bring the inner him to the surface so she could finally, *truly,* meet him.

There was no hesitation in his writing. No fear of what would she think. He simply opened up and allowed his heart to bleed onto the paper.

Grace spent the rest of the afternoon curled up on the couch with the letters from John to her mom in her lap. She had reread most of them. The man that had showed up at her house earlier was the man in the letters, no doubt. She had seen that side of him. She thought back to her childhood and how cold the man had been every time she ran into him.

She had kept her distance from him knowing only bits and pieces of the feud from other people. Her mom never said a word about it. Whenever Grace questioned her, her mom would change the subject. Near as Grace could figure, it had gone on for a few generations, with the Stevens family always feeling they were better than everyone else. She never understood it, but it always came down to social class, and the Stevens were high society with old money. The Robinson's, Abigail's family name, was working class and never could break that barrier. Grace never saw her mom show any animosity towards the Stevens, and now Grace knew why. She was the epitome of rising above.

Grace smiled. Her mom's favorite expression had always been, "Rise above the difficult situations. You will see it differently from a higher view." Grace now understood. Was this the reason her mom put Xander and her in this situation? Just to show her understanding through difficulty? Grace sighed. Even from the grave, Mom kept teaching her lessons.

Time seemed to freeze as Grace closed her eyes and allowed her thoughts to drift to her mom and the memories of her childhood. Visions of her father and mother dancing in the kitchen, happy moments through her life with holidays, negated any thoughts that her parents hadn't been happy. She knew they were in every fiber of her being.

She startled from her dreams with the closing of the front door. She focused her eyes as Xander walked into the living room.

"Everything okay?" Xander gestured towards the letters in her lap.

"They make me feel closer to Mom." Grace straightened the letters and put them back in the box.

She started to move her legs when Xander made towards the couch, but he caught her legs and put them across his lap as he sat down. He gently started rubbing her feet and she couldn't help but relax and enjoy his touch.

"Where've you been?"

"Went for a ride to the lighthouse to clear my mind." Xander's hands stilled. "I know things have been a bit stilted between us, but I want to get past that."

"We're okay. It's just been a lot of stress. We're just dealing with it in our own way, that's all." Grace wiggled her foot against his hand. "Feel free to keep those hands going."

A chuckle escaped Xander and Grace smiled. She closed her eyes and lay back, allowing Xander to work his magic on her feet. For the moment, the comfortable silence was all they needed. Grace struggled with whether or not to tell Xander about his dad's visit and in the end, she held her tongue. It wasn't necessary to go into it. If she knew Xander at all, he would be more irritated than pleased at the news.

Not wanting to push his luck, Xander excused himself to his room shortly after dinner. They had kept the compatibleness between them through dinner. He was anxious to put his plan in motion in the morning, but for now he needed some space. All he could think about was pulling her into his arms and kissing her senseless and teasing her with his fingers until she begged for more.

Xander settled onto his bed, his back propped against a pillow. He read and reread his writings from earlier. As he worked on rewriting it, he paused and smiled. This was him. Grace would finally have a glimpse into who he really was.

It felt good to finally open up.

Chapter Thirty

Grace wandered to the kitchen. It had been a long, sleepless night. She stumbled as she, willed the coffee maker to already have her magic brew ready. As she neared the counter, she found a full of coffee and an envelope with her name on it in front of the coffee maker. The coffee was hot. Xander obviously had heard her coming and poured her coffee fresh. She closed her eyes and inhaled the rich aroma before taking her first sip.

He was forever thoughtful, doing little things that just blew her away. He had no idea how much she appreciated these small gestures and how much it chipped away at the wall that she struggled to keep in place whenever he was around. She glanced at the envelope again and wondered what it could be. She continued sipping her coffee, delaying the opening of the envelope. She feared bad news, but she was curious.

She finally set her coffee aside and grabbed it. She turned it over and opened it slowly. Pulling a single piece of paper out, she opened it and started to read.

I sit…Not in my own skin, not in my own space.

I don't know, what, where, or when.

My God! I thought I was in control of my heart, my world.

I sit…Watching the waves ebb and flow with relentless timeless repetition.

The ebb is peaceful, calm and unassuming.

Flow crashes into my chest, my heart, my being

You were guarded by your existence and your place in the planet.

Stoic and unknowingly steadfast.

Hardened early in life, complacent

I will be a gentle breeze grazing your shoulder,

Caressing the tiniest hairs on your neck that can only be witnessed

When the afternoon sun shines from a waning day low in the sky.

Your head will tilt. questioning the moment, yet no one is there.

Wave after wave, tide after tide, you will realize my presence as a constant.

You are safe...Safe with me. Pure.

Grace closed her eyes. She felt the hotness of tears as they escaped from under her lashes and ran down her cheeks. The simple words had in an instance shattered the wall she had built around her heart. She opened her eyes and reread the words again. Her heartbeat as if it had awakened from a long sleep, slow and steady, yet with an anticipation that Grace had never experienced. His words rang true, and for once her fear had dissipated, leaving her with a yearning for more.

It was like meeting Xander for the first time. The words painted a clear picture as to who he was and his capacity for love. She carefully moved the paper aside so her tears, flowing heavily now, would not stain the paper and blur the words. Sobs ripped through her as if an ice dam had finally let go. She knew without a doubt she loved this man, but she would be damned if she knew what she was supposed to do next. Her first instinct was to hide away and not face him at all, knowing he would expect some sort of response from her. Her response at this moment was purely animalistic and she just wanted to feel his body next to hers, his heart to beat with hers as they allowed their love to finally come together. She carefully refolded the paper and slid it into the envelope. She carried it upstairs, holding it against her heart.

Grace lay on her bed, holding close the envelope. She needed to feel it physically against her. The words were so potent she was having trouble processing it all. The emotion flowed so heavily through the words. Grace struggled to catch her breath just thinking of those words she had read in the kitchen. She was torn—torn between wanting to find Xander and have him hold her, or running away and never allow her heart to feel this way. It hurt almost physically from the need of wanting that love that was being so freely given by Xander.

She pulled out the paper and reread the words one more time. The tears started to flow again and she closed her eyes and sobbed for all that she had missed already and all that she had held herself from because of her fear. Was it too late to have this?

Chapter Thirty-One

Xander drove into the driveway and found the Police Chief just starting up the stairs to the front door. He turned at the sound of the motorcycle and waited for Xander to approach.

"What's going on, Chief?" Xander approached and shook the chief's hand.

"Xander, just the person I was looking for."

"What's up?" Xander leaned against the railing of the porch. "Progress in who set the fire?"

The Chief shook his head and cleared his throat. "I do need you to come downtown with me though."

"What's going on?"

"I have some questions for you."

"Come in and I'll be happy to answer."

The Chief stepped down a step. "I think we should do this at the station."

"Why?" A cold chill ran through Xander.

"Please, Xander, let's not make this more difficult than it needs to be." The Chief frowned.

Xander shrugged. "I have nothing to hide. Can I let Grace know?"

The Chief nodded. "She might want to come. I'll need you to ride with me."

Xander headed up the stairs to Grace's room, "Grace?"

He heard the sobs quiet and he stood just outside the door, giving her some time. "What do you want?"

"Fire chief is here." Xander pushed the door open wider. "Are you okay?"

Grace turned towards him, wiping her tears away. Her eyes were red from the tears she had shed. "Yes, I'm fine." She stood from her bed and slid an envelope onto her nightstand.

Xander recognized the envelope, but said nothing. He hadn't intended to make her cry. His heart felt like it ripped apart as his eyes met hers.

"Go ahead down. I'll be right there." She gave him a small smile.

"Meet me at the Police Station. Chief wants me to go down there with him to answer some questions."

Grace stared at him. "Why?" Her voice shook and Xander felt her doubt penetrating the room.

"I don't know.

The ride to the police station was quiet. Xander sat in the back seat of the police cruiser feeling like a criminal and wondering why he was being treated this way. The Chief kept glancing at him in the rearview mirror, but looking away every time Xander met his eyes.

He was furious. He had done nothing and this was ridiculous. The doubt that was evident in Grace before he left the house sliced Xander to the core. He was led into an interrogation room. Xander remained silent as he slid into a chair and waited for the Chief to sit down across from him.

"Xander, I'm sorry. It's just routine procedure." The Chief gave a half smile, trying to break the ice.

"Routine procedure? Treating me like I did something wrong?" Xander shook his head.

"Just a few questions and then I'm sure Grace will be here to pick you up. It won't take long."

Xander nodded. This was the reason he never put down roots, never stayed in one spot long enough to be accused of anything – and he didn't do much. He kept his nose in his own business and never started trouble. He learned his lesson from Abigail. She had taught him to stay clean and he could stay away from the trouble. It had worked – until now.

He waited, silently. There was no reason to be agitated, or at least no reason to show his agitation.

"One of my men found a jacket behind the barn. We took it and bagged it for evidence, but I've got to say…there was a name in the jacket, on the tag."

"Whose name?" Xander voice as soft, but icy.

"Stevens." The chief made eye contact. "Do you know anything about it?"

Xander shook his head. "I'm not missing a jacket and I don't put my name on my clothes. God, do you think someone is trying to frame me?" Disbelief ran through him. *Who would do this to him?*

The Chief shrugged his shoulders. "You have to know how this looks. You never wanted to be back in this town and Abigail put you in quite a spot keeping you here."

"I would never do anything to ruin Grace's chances of her inheritance." Xander shook his head.

"And what do you know about where I want to put my roots down? People change, grow up, circumstances..." Xander ran his fingers through his hair.

Grace had been slow to follow Xander to the police station. Her mind reeled with why the police wanted to question him. Fear gripped her. She berated herself for starting to open her heart to Xander and now this. How could she have fallen for him and his charm? She cleared her mind as she parked and started into the station. They had been expecting her, she realized when she was ushered into a conference room to wait for the chief.

Thankfully, she didn't have to wait long with her wandering mind before a young officer came in.

"Can I get you anything?"

Grace shook her head. "Where's Xander?"

"He's still talking with the chief, but they should be wrapping it up soon." He settled into the chair across from her.

"What's this all about?"

The officer smiled. "Chief will answer your questions soon."

Grace stood and paced the small room. There was nothing more she hated than to be cooped up in a confined space. Minutes passed, although they seemed like an hour, and Grace forced herself to stay calm when the door finally opened and in walked the chief and Xander.

"Grace, sorry to keep you waiting." Chief held out his hand to shake hers. Grace gripped it briefly and nodded.

"Do I get to find out what's going on?"

"We can talk about it at home." Xander turned towards the chief. "I am free to go now, right?"

"Yes, of course. Thank you for being so cooperative." Chief nodded and stepped aside so Grace and Xander could pass through the door. "Please stay close, Xander. We might have a few more questions."

Grace's glance flitted between the chief and Xander. She felt she definitely missed something and was anxious to get Xander to the car to quiz him on what was going on.

Once they were situated in the car and Grace had started it, she turned towards home. She tried to calm her thoughts, putting together in her mind what she wanted to say when truthfully all she wanted to do was let him have it for causing so much turmoil in her life.

"Well?" She had no other words.

"They found a jacket and apparently it had 'Stevens' in it so they questioned me about it being mine." Xander shrugged.

Fury raged through Grace at his blasé attitude. "What do you know about this?"

"Nothing." Xander met her eyes and uncertainty shone from them. "Gracie, please believe me."

"I don't know what to believe." She was silent the rest of the ride, not trusting herself to speak. Fear rose in her. *Mother, what did you get me into?*

Finally arriving home, Grace bolted from the car and raced into the house. Xander caught up with her as she crossed the threshold into the foyer. Xander grabbed her hand and pulled her close as he stood and wrapped his free arm around her.

"You know deep down I had nothing to do with this." His words were spoken softly against her forehead. He felt the struggle going on within her as she stayed stiff in his arms, trying to fight what it was that was between them. He pressed a soft kiss to her forehead, another to each of her eyes. "It kills me to see you cry."

"I'm not crying," she stated, though her eyes closed as she leaned against him. He felt the stress lift from her as she became soft and yielding to him. He let go of her wrist he had been holding and ran his hand up her side to pull her closer.

"I love you, Grace." The words were barely a whisper, but she nodded as she heard them. Although he couldn't see her, he felt her stiffen slightly before relaxing again. He pulled back just a little so he could search her eyes. "Look at me." The command was spoken with such gentleness, but she obeyed immediately.

"I need to know you are okay." She nodded briefly, tears shimmering on her eyelashes as she fought to hold on to what little control she seemed to have.

"I'm fine."

"Gracie...it's me. I can see you're not fine. I never wanted to hurt you. I only...I was just trying to express how you make me feel."

She looked up and stared into his eyes. "I know. I'm not hurt. I just don't know...what I'm feeling right now." She reached up and laid the palm of her hand against his cheek. "Just let me sort it out."

He pulled her closer, his lips claiming hers. She sighed softly and gave into the moment. He allowed himself the pleasure of her surrender, kissing him back, as a good sign. The doorbell ringing pulled them apart and Grace glanced up to meet his eyes.

"What now?"

Xander squeezed her hand gently as he started for the door. Grace followed him to the living room entrance and waited. Xander swung up the door and took a step back.

"Hello, Sebastian…Xander."

Fury flooded through Grace as she heard John's voice. She blocked out Xander's response and took two steps into the foyer just as John closed the door behind him.

"You! Impeccable timing you have." Grace stood, hands on her hips, anger coming off her in waves. "Did you come to tie up loose ends with your son?"

Xander turned and stared at Grace. "What are you talking about?"

John placed a hand on his son's arm. "I'm here to try and mend fences with my son, if that is what you mean."

"Oh, please. You two have been scheming behind my back. How long have you been planning to drive me out of my home?" Grace took a deep breath, trying to calm herself. "Newsflash, Xander doesn't get anything without me being here. What do you get if we don't get Mom's property? You think you can swoop in and buy it up for yourself? It will go to charity first."

Grace felt the blood rush to her face. Her heart pounded and its beating filled her ears until she thought she was going to explode.

"Grace, you don't believe that." Xander's voice was full of despair. He couldn't lose her, not like this.

"Are you insane?" Xander clamped his mouth shut, a look of panic crossing his face.

"Yes, Sebastian, I'm insane...a raving lunatic. You better watch out because God knows what I am capable of." Xander stepped back involuntarily as if he had been slapped.

Grace heard the shrillness of her words and saw Xander's face pale with the use of his given name. She knew deep down she was being unreasonable, but she couldn't stop it. She feared the madness from the stress was returning and running rampart. She had to get out of here.

She pushed past Xander and John, storming out of the house with a slam of the door behind her. She ran to her car and as soon as the door shut, she laid her forehead against the steering wheel. Tears overflowed her eyes. She struggled with trying to hold them back, and finally gave in to the sobs that wracked her body. She couldn't hold on to this anymore. She didn't want to lose her home, but she couldn't be in the same house one more minute with Xander if he was determined to destroy her.

She was too fragile for this. She longed to get back to the moment he walked into her life and she felt that she could be someone else. The moment when he spurred a freedom in her that she couldn't resist after fighting for it all her life.

Pulling herself up and glancing around, Grace started her car and turned towards town. This was going to have to stop, and the only way to do it was to admit defeat herself. She wiped her tears away as she drove and mentally gave herself a pep talk. She could convince herself that her old life was what she wanted and that she could go back to it with no problems, forgetting Xander and everything he had given her. If nothing else, she would have the poem he had written her. With a sigh, she realized she had become her mother. Giving in and keeping mementos of memories of good moments, and yet letting go of the man who had changed her life.

She parked in front of Bob's office. She entered it and took a deep breath.

"Ms. McAllister, did you have an appointment?"

Grace shook her head. "No, but is Bob available? This will only take a moment."

Grace slipped into a chair as the secretary picked up the phone to talk to her boss. Bob must have agreed as within minutes his door opened.

"Grace, what a pleasant surprise. Come on in."

Grace entered and sat down on the edge of a chair. She waited while Bob settled back into his chair behind the desk. She met his eyes. She hesitated, trying to form the words that needed to be said. The longer Bob sat in silence waiting for her to start, the more irritated she became. She stood abruptly and paced the office.

"Do you want to tell me what's going on?" Bob finally broke the silence.

"I can't do this." Defeat ran through Grace, bringing her shoulders down. She was shrouded in sadness.

"Can't do what?" Bob gestured to the chair. "Please, Grace, sit down."

Grace stumbled back to the chair and sank into it, her posture spent and fatigue setting in. "This business with Xander, trying to hold on to Mom's home...all of it."

"It's *your* home, Grace, not Abigail's." Bob sat back with a small smile on his face.

"Of course it's not. Not unless we manage to pull off all her stipulations."

"Right." Bob leaned forward and stared at Grace. "Is it the business you are having a hard time getting started, or is it the realization that you are in love with Xander that is bothering you?"

Grace lifted her head and stared at him. "Love with Xander? Of course I'm not in love with him."

"Oh, okay."

Grace closed her eyes. "I can't be in love with him. He's, he's trying to sabotage everything." Grace filled Bob in on the jacket that had been found and how John had out of the blue arrived to talk with his son. "It's all just too coincidental to be by accident."

"Hmmm, well, have you talked to Xander about it?"

"What's to talk about?" Grace sighed. "He's an enigma. One minute he is supportive and wants to do anything to keep the house, and the next he is doing things to ruin any chance I have."

"Yes, love is messy that way."

"What are you talking about? He says he loves me, but…"

Bob stood and walked around to sit in the chair next to Grace. "But what? Grace, I can see that he loves you. Can't you?"

"He says it, and sometimes I feel it, but I don't know…it scares me." Grace turned to face Bob. "What if I'm having blackouts again and I am going insane?"

Bob chuckled. "Not happening. You got past that and yes, you are under some stress, but you have got to trust your heart. You love him or you wouldn't be this upset by all of this."

"I don't know how to love him. I can't give him what he needs."

"What is that? A man in love just needs the love returned to him. There is no hidden agenda." Bob patted her hand. "Think about it. Love has been around since the beginning of time. There is no instruction manual, but you can't run from it. Not if you ever want to be truly happy."

Grace lowered her chin. "I don't know what to think, or feel. It's all so new, the thought of actually falling in love with someone."

"Thought of falling in love, or the fact that you have fallen and you never saw it coming?" Bob pulled Grace to her feet. "Don't overthink it, Grace. Just allow yourself to feel and things will fall into place as they should be."

Grace nodded. She turned to leave and stopped at the door. "Thanks Bob. Please keep this conversation between us. I'm not ready for Xander to know."

After leaving Bob's office, Grace turned towards the coast and drove. Time passed quickly as she let her thoughts wander as she traveled along the coastal route. Pulling into the small restaurant where Xander had taken her the first time they had gone for a motorcycle ride, she stared out the windshield at the waves crashing on the rocks. She allowed herself to feel the emotions that she had been fighting for the past few days, weeks, since Xander walked into her life. A peace settled around her as she granted herself permission to admit she loved him.

Chapter Thirty-Two

Xander flinched with the slam of the door behind Grace. He turned on his father, hands in fists at his side.

"What the hell have you done?"

"I haven't done anything." John stood his ground. "Maybe I should ask you the same question. Grace seems to think you are involved in this."

Xander ran his fingers through his hair and sighed. "I know she thinks I'm involved and things are pointing that way, but it's not me. Who wants to frame me for this? The estate will go to charity, like she said, if we don't fulfill our obligations as set by Abigail."

Xander turned towards the living room. He placed his hands on the mantel of the fireplace and closed his eyes. "I don't know how I can fix this."

He heard his father move about the room and finally sat down. Xander turned to look at him. "Why are you here, Father?"

"I'm here because after talking with Grace the other day, I realized how much I have messed up our relationship and I want to make amends."

Xander snorted. "Make amends? You threw me away like an old rag."

John shook his head. "It wasn't like that. I kept tabs on you through Abigail all these years. I have been so proud of you and yet my own pride got in the way of my telling you that."

"Why all of a sudden do you feel the need to 'mend bridges?' What's in it for you?" Xander paced. "We both know you never do anything without an ulterior motive."

John sighed. "Yes, it's true in the past every move I made was based on what I could get from it. It's not like that this time, Sebas….Xander. I'm trying and I really want to make things right. There are things you just don't know about your mother's and my marriage, about things that happened that forced me to send you away."

"Forced you to send me away? Really?" Xander scoffed.

"I was a coward back then, to a point I still am. You are the strongest person I know and I'm amazed by the integrity you show now and have shown over the years."

Xander sat down. "Words are cheap, so forgive me for not believing a thing you are trying to sell right now. I really think you should go."

John stood. "I'm sorry. I'm not going to stop trying and maybe one day I will earn a chance to make those amends with you."

Xander stayed in the chair, hearing the door shut behind his father. Emotions flooded him. Words he had wanted to hear all his life had just been said to him and yet he couldn't forgive him – not yet. There was an unfamiliar sharpness in his heart that threatened to bring forth those insecurities from his childhood, threatened to crack his wall he had built up around him when it came to his father. He vowed a long time ago that the man would never hurt him again, yet hearing those words from him had hurt.

Xander had no idea how much time had passed when he heard the door open. Without turning around, he sensed Grace standing in the doorway, watching him. He wanted to go to her and hold her close, to give both of them some comfort. He needed comfort from her and yet he didn't want to feel that weak to need so much from someone else. He had hardened himself to those needs years ago.

"I'm back." Grace's words were no more than a whisper and he heard her footsteps head towards the stairs. He said nothing and just continued to sit there. Fear gripped his heart. Would she walk away from him forever? He didn't care about the inheritance, but he didn't want to live without her in his life.

Time continued until the shadows deepened in the living room. He glanced around and realized that he had missed dinner – Grace obviously had not come back downstairs to eat either. He sighed and stood to head to bed. The loneliness overwhelmed him.

Xander tossed and turned as the clock continued to tick by minute by minute, hour by hour. At three-thirty his stomach began to protest the fact that he had skipped dinner. With a growl, he threw back the covers and started for the stairs.

He paused at the top of the staircase, hearing sounds coming from the kitchen. Grace must have gotten hungry too. He hesitated, wanting to give her space, but his stomach rumbled again and he knew there was no choice but to go get some food.

He crept to the kitchen and hesitated by the door before pushing it open. Seeing her back to him, it took a second to register this was not Grace. Just as it clicked, the man turned to face Xander.

Xander on instinct ran to block the back door and got there just before the other man did. "Who are you?"

The man smiled and leaned against the counter. "Don't recognize me, bro?"

Dale. He hadn't seen his brother in years and now here he was standing in front of him. "What are you doing here?"

"Came for a visit...well, not really, but I heard you were doing quite well for yourself. Wanted to see with my own eyes."

Xander clenched his fists at his side. "So you broke into my house?"

"Well, breaking in is such a strong term. Why don't we call it visiting you?"

Xander shook his head. "You're not visiting in the middle of the night when everyone else is asleep." Xander slipped his hand into his pocket.

His fingers closed around his cell phone. "Are you missing a jacket?"

Dale's laughter filled the kitchen. "I must have dropped it in the hurry to get away. You and your girlfriend found the fire a little too quickly. Must have been up already?"

Xander pulled out the cell phone and punched in 9-1-1.

"Come on, bro, no need to call the police." Dale stood straight and took a step towards Xander.

When the line picked up, Xander said, "I'd like to report a break in. Yes, that's the address. He's still here." Xander quickly answered a few more questions.

"I'll be leaving now." Dale tried to push past Xander to the door. Xander dropped the phone, and instincts kicked in. He immediately laid Dale flat out on his back with a right hook under the chin. Dale struggled for a second before slipping into unconsciousness.

Xander reached for the phone again. "Yes, I'm still here. He's unconscious at the moment, but he did confirm starting the fire in the barn also."

Xander grabbed some rope from a drawer in the kitchen and tied Dale's hands together. He went and unlocked the front door. After checking on Dale one more time and seeing he was still unconscious, he ran up the stairs and knocked on Grace's door.

"Grace, get up." He pushed the door open and called to her again.

"What is it?" Grace sat up, clenching the sheet to her chest.

"We've got company. Police are on the way. Get dressed and come downstairs." Xander turned and left before she replied.

Xander had ushered the police into the kitchen before Grace put in an appearance. He kept his eyes on her as she glanced around the bustling kitchen, bewildered. Dale had awakened and was now in handcuffs, glaring at Xander.

Xander walked over to Grace. "Glad you could join us."

"What is going on?" Grace turned to face Xander. "And who is that?"

Xander sighed. His family certainly had a way of barging into his life and he knew there would be more accusations forthcoming. "That's my brother, Dale. I came to the kitchen for something to eat and caught him in the house."

"In the house!" Grace turned towards the group of officers and Dale over by the door. "What does he want?"

"Miss, can I ask you a few questions?" A police officer approached.

Grace nodded, not taking her eyes of Dale.

"Why don't we step out of the kitchen here?" The officer gestured her into the foyer and Grace walked ahead of him.

"What is going on?" She turned abruptly, causing the police officer to stop short.

"Miss, do you know that man?"

Grace tapped her foot against the floor. "I was just told it was Xander's brother. I don't remember him."

"Okay. Do you have any idea why he would be in your kitchen?"

Grace scoffed. "How should I know? Maybe you should do your job and ask him why he is here."

The man snapped shut his notebook. "I'm just trying to get all the information I can, miss."

"Look, there has been an abundance of stuff going on around here and it all seems to be centered around the Stevens' family. Start there and figure it out." Grace stormed past the police officer and entered the kitchen, searching for Xander.

She met his eyes and blinked quickly to stop the tears that threatened. When she was able to clear her vision, Xander stood in front of her.

"You okay?"

Grace glanced up into his eyes. "No, I'm not okay. What is going on? Why is your family screwing with my life?"

"I swear to you, I have no idea what is going on." Xander glanced over his shoulder at his brother. "I didn't even know where Dale was. I haven't seen him in years."

"Okay. But why is he here and what is he doing? Did he start the fire?" Realization hit Grace hard. "He did, didn't he?"

Xander nodded. He didn't have a choice but to tell her the truth. A truth that somehow he felt was implicating him just by association.

"Why?" Tears overflowed her lashes, spilling down her cheeks. She cried unchecked, allowing all the stress of the past few weeks to flow from her.

Xander pulled her into his arms and held her close. No words were needed. He willed his strength to her and hoped and prayed she would accept it.

Chapter Thirty-Three

Grace stood watching the coffee maker brew the magical juice she was counting on to wake her up. She had been up since early morning and still had more questions than answers. Dale had been hauled away and now Xander and she were alone in the house once again.

Xander had gone to shower while Grace made coffee. The black brew dripping into the carafe mesmerized her. She tried to figure out what she had done to deserve this unlikely turn of events.

Xander had denied knowing anything about his brother being in the area, and yet something nagged at Grace. She realized she didn't know anything about Xander or his family. In the time they had spent trying to get to know each other, he never talked much about his family or his childhood, only of the recent past and his present.

Just one more reason to justify the fact that she couldn't be in love with Xander – she knew nothing about him. And if her mother had taught her anything, it was to be cautious and not jump into anything without all the facts. Yet as hard as she tried to convince herself of the fact she didn't love him, in her heart she knew it wasn't true. He had worked his way into her heart and as much as she tried to deny it, she was heads over heels in love with that man.

She groaned just as the coffee maker beeped. signaling it was ready. "Perfect timing." Xander's voice behind her broke through her thoughts.

She poured coffee into two mugs and doctored them up. Ironically, they took their coffee the same way and it comforted her somehow to realize this. She handed a mug to Xander.

"Thanks."

She nodded and moved to the window in the kitchen, looking out to the barn. "We need to decide what we're going to do."

Xander slid onto a stool. "I thought we already did."

Grace turned to face him. "I know you think we can just continue on with the business, but everything is behind schedule now."

"Yup, it's behind schedule. We roll with it and continue on."

Grace closed her eyes as she sipped her coffee. He made it sound so easy. "What about Dale?"

Xander set his mug down. "What about him? He goes to jail. I don't really care about what happens to him, Gracie. I only care about us." He stood and walked over to her. Reaching for her, he placed his hands on her hips. "Do you want the business?"

"I don't know what I want. I don't want to let Mom down, but it seems impossible." Grace set her mug down. "At least I'm not crazy." She muttered.

"Crazy? What are you talking about?"

"With everything being moved around, I thought I was doing it and not remembering. I was taking bets on the fact that I must be losing my mind."

Xander smiled. "You're a little crazy, but not in that way."

Grace smiled weakly up at him. "You know what I mean."

He nodded, stepping back away from her to lean against the bar. "What do you want to do, Grace? Do you want to work towards the inheritance or do you want to give up on it?"

"Are those the only choices?" Grace dropped her head. "I don't know. Part of me wants it, because this is home. It's where I grew up. Parts of me and Mom are here. But then another part wants to live my own life without feeling like Mom is still telling me what to do, calling the shots at every turn." Frustration laced her words.

Xander folded his arms across his chest. "I'm leaving the decision to you. I want you, Gracie. You whether you are here and we have an inheritance together or whether it is you as a school teacher living in your small apartment. I love you and I'm not leaving no matter what you decide."

He turned and grabbed his coffee mug. Refilling it, he glanced at her with a gesture for more coffee. She held out her mug and watched him fill it. Warmth spread through her as she heard those words again. *He wasn't going anywhere.* She just needed to decide if she wanted the house, this house with Xander, or if she wanted to start a life outside of here with him.

She stood there long after he left the room, the words of his poem going through her mind. She had memorized it already. She wanted to deny it one more time, but couldn't. She loved him. There was really only one thing to do.

Grace finished her coffee and rinsed her cup. She turned towards the back yard and proceeded towards the barn. She walked around the place. It had been cleaned up for the most part – ashes shoveled and raked, the area cleared and ready for rebuilding. Wood had been delivered and things were in place. Grace knew it could be done within a couple of weeks. In reality, their schedule was only delayed slightly. She once again hesitated and doubted her decision she had made just a few minutes before in the kitchen.

She sighed when it dawned on her that she really didn't know what she wanted and as much as she could try and fool herself, no decision had been made.

"I thought I might find you here. Police called. Dale wants to talk. Didn't know if you wanted to take a ride with me?" Xander spoke quietly.

Grace turned to face him. "What does he want to talk about?"

"I don't know. But it could be interesting." Xander held out his hand to her. "You up for it?"

She nodded and took his hand. Xander laced his fingers through hers and walked silently beside her.

"Everything is ready for the work on the barn to start tomorrow." Grace spoke out loud, although speaking more to herself.

"Yes."

She glanced at him. "Don't you have any opinion at all on what we should do?"

He stopped and turned towards her. "It's your decision, Grace. I want what you want."

She started walking again. "It's not that simple."

"It can be if you just trust your gut." Xander squeezed her hand and handed her a helmet from the back of his bike. There was no more talk between them as they rode into town. Grace welcomed the silence and leaned against Xander's back as her mind wandered. He oozed strength and compassion, never once telling her what he wanted. She hugged close to his back and enjoyed the movement as one between them on the bike.

When Xander parked in front of the police station, Grace was slow to loosen her grip. He sat waiting for her, and yet he just rested his hand on her arm. There was no gesture to hurry her, just a simple understanding of the war that raged within her and allowing her to battle it in her own time.

"Ready?" Grace sat back and lifted her helmet from her head.

Xander nodded and waited for her to get off the bike. After securing the helmets, he turned and with his hand at the small of her back, he guided her into the station.

They were greeted by an officer who directed them to the detective's office who had been handling the case. He was expecting them and had put Dale in one of the integration rooms. Xander stopped Grace just outside the door. "You sure you want to do this with me?"

Grace nodded. They entered the room and took chairs across the table from Dale.

"Well, well. I didn't expect your girlfriend to show up, too." Dale smirked at Grace.

"You wanted to talk. Say what you have to and get it over with." Xander slammed his hand down on the table, getting Dale's attention back to himself.

"Fine. Look, I need to be bailed out." Dale sat forward. "You help me out, I'll help you."

"What could you do to help us? You caused this whole mess." Grace's hard voice obviously took Dale by surprise and he sat back.

"I have information." Dale kept his eyes on Xander.

Xander reached out and placed his hand on Grace's arm. "What kind of information?"

"You didn't think I did this alone, did you?" Dale grinned. "You give me more credit than I deserve, my dear brother."

Xander fought the urge to knock the grin off Dale's face and took a deep breath, praying he could stay calm. "Well, who is the mastermind behind all this?"

Dale shook his head. "Nope. We need an agreement first."

"I'm not bailing you out. You were trespassing, you vandalized my house..." Xander pushed his chair back and stood.

"Your house. That's interesting. I thought it wasn't yours until two years were up and that was only after completing what the old bag wanted you to do."

Grace stood beside Xander. "That 'old bag,' as you put it, was my mother. And I don't know where you got your information, but it is wrong." Grace pushed gently against Xander's arm. He glanced down at her and nodded. They turned and left the room, leaving Dale staring after them openmouthed.

The detective waited outside the room. "He didn't give up any information. Why did you leave?"

Xander turned towards Grace and waited for her to answer.

"He has information, sure, but he's not ready to talk quite yet. I think we'll go grab some lunch and then will come back later. Let him sit and think for a bit." Grace smiled at the detective. "Say about an hour, hour and a half we'll be back?"

The detective nodded. Grace looped her arm through Xander's and glanced up. "Hungry, dear?"

Xander smiled and nodded. She was up to something and he liked it.

Chapter Thirty-Four

Grace and Xander settled into the local diner and perused the menus. Xander set his aside and watched Grace. Her lips pursed as she debated on what she wanted to get. When she finally set the menu aside and glanced up, he did all he could not to laugh out loud.

"What?"

"Quite a production in deciding what you want."

She stuck out her tongue at him. "Everything is so good here. I always have a hard time deciding what I'm going to have."

The chit chat died down as the waitress appeared and took their orders. Grace played with her fork as she watched Xander. "Do you think Dale is telling the truth? That someone else is behind all this?"

"I suppose he could be. I can't imagine who it would be, though." Xander pondered carefully before saying any more. "I don't want you to get upset by things he says about Abigail. You know he is acting out because of the relationship I had with her."

Grace nodded. "What exactly was your relationship with her?"

"She was more of a mother to me than my own ever was. She took an interest in things I did. Got me out of trouble and encouraged me to make something out of myself. I guess I would say she was my mentor."

"Sounds like Mom. Always taking in strays." Grace's hand rose quickly to cover her mouth. "I didn't mean it like that."

Xander chuckled. "I know. It's true in some ways, though."

As the food appeared in front of them, they ate in silence. After they had eaten and checked the time, they decided to take a stroll to the park in town and just relax while Dale stewed some more.

Xander was convinced that Grace had probably found the right button to push by making him wait. A tactic he never would have thought to use. They walked in silence, a comfortable silence that Grace found warming. She allowed herself to feel the possibility of what life would be like with Xander by herself, the possibility of telling him that she really did love him. But it wasn't a conversation she was ready to have with him and she allowed fear to overrule her desire to share her heart's desires with Xander.

Fear could be a powerful motivator, Grace realized. She stopped walking and turned to Xander. "What would Dale be the most afraid of?"

Xander shook his head. "What do you mean?"

Grace pulled Xander to a nearby bench. "Fear. It motivates us. What would Dale be most afraid of that would have pushed him into doing this?"

"I don't know. Grace, I haven't talked to my brother since we were kids. I don't have any idea what he is like now, what motivates him to do things."

"Okay, but most fears that we have carry over from our childhood. What was he like as a child?" Grace asked.

Xander sat back and stared into space. "I don't know. We weren't close growing up. Mother couldn't stand the sight of me and well, Dale spent all his time trying to please her."

Grace clapped her hands together. "That's it!"

"What is?" Xander turned toward her.

"Your mother has to be the key to all this."

Xander shook his head. "My mother is a cold heartless woman, but I don't think she would go this far."

Grace stood and reached for Xander's hand. "Well, let's go find out what Dale has to say, shall we?"

They strolled arm in arm toward the police station with Grace humming softly. Xander smiled at her sudden spark of excitement. This would be interesting, to say the least.

The detective met them outside of the interrogation room. "He has been a bundle of nerves since you left. Pacing, muttering to himself. He asked to make a phone call, but since it wasn't to a lawyer he wasn't granted that. Put him in a foul mood." He turned towards Grace. "I hope you know what you're doing."

Grace patted his arm. "We'll find out, won't we?"

Xander shrugged at the detective and opened the door to allow Grace to precede him into the room.

"Where did you go?" Dale stopped his pacing and turned to face Xander and Grace as they entered the room.

"Doesn't matter." Xander held the chair for Grace before sitting himself. "Let's talk."

"Now you want to talk. What if I don't want to anymore?" Dale leaned on the back of the empty chair in the room.

"Then don't talk, but I'm not going to waste my time here unless you've got something to say." Xander gave him a charming smile.

Dale glanced between Grace and Xander. She didn't say a word to him, just sat there staring back. Xander gestured to the chair. "Are you going to sit and talk?"

Dale slid into the chair. "I need to be bailed out."

"That's not going to happen until I hear what you have to say and then I'll decide if it is worthwhile or not."

Dale fidgeted and tapped his fingers on the table. "At least, get them to let me make a phone call." He nodded over his shoulder towards the door.

"Who you calling?"

Dale shrugged. "Mother. She'll bail me out."

Xander snorted. "Of course. I should have known. She has always bailed you out of trouble, hasn't she?"

Dale sat forward, elbows on the table, "Well, we didn't all have an old bag at our beck and call."

"Really? Looks like you are still calling yours." Xander clenched his teeth as soon as the words left his mouth. He couldn't be dragged down to his brother's, hell, half brother's level.

Dale laughed. "You just don't get it, do you?"

"Enlighten me."

"You made things worse for yourself by allowing that woman into your life, and the fact that Father kept in touch with her all these years. It was a slap in the face to Mother. She deserved better."

Xander stood. "I doubt she deserved better than what she drained from Father, but I'm done with this conversation."

Grace continued to sit and glanced up at Xander. He raised his eyebrow at her and she shook her head no slightly. With a sigh, Xander sat back down.

"Dale, tell me, why are you so afraid of her?" Grace's voice broke the strained silence and Dale met her eyes.

"Afraid of who? Your mother?"

Grace smiled. "No, yours."

"I'm not afraid of her." Dale's words were hesitant.

"No? Okay, why are you still striving for her approval then?"

Dale slammed his hand down. "Look, bro, get her outta here. She has no business in this."

Grace stood. "Actually I do. It was *my* property you vandalized."

Xander stood. "We're through. Good luck getting out of this one."

Grace and Xander were met by the detective as soon as they left the room. "Not much to go on."

"How much do you need? He already admitted to starting the fire and he was caught in the house." Xander took a deep breath. "Look I don't want any more contact with him. Call his mother to come make bail."

The detective nodded. "Well, that's the funny thing. She states she doesn't want anything to do with him and to let him rot in jail, and I quote, like his father."

"Who's his real father?" Grace asked.

The detective tipped his head towards her. "Excuse me? John Stevens isn't his father?"

"No, he's not." Xander grabbed Grace's elbow and steered her towards the door.

"What are you doing?" Grace hissed as they left the station.

"I want answers before that nosy detective starts digging around my family. We're going to my parents' house."

"Do you really want to do this?" Grace had insisted they go back to the house first and talk. She watched Xander pace the living room and prayed he knew what he was doing.

"Don't you want to know why Dale did this?" Xander demanded.

Grace shrugged. "Does it matter really why he did it? He did it and now we are starting over." Grace curled her legs up under her on the couch. She had done a lot of thinking while sitting in the police station listening to Dale spew his bitterness over Xander and Abigail's relationship. He was a hurting man, and most of it wasn't his fault. Grace was angry for the part he played, but she knew from her own experience that sometimes forces beyond your control influenced your path.

"Why do you not care all of a sudden?" Xander stopped pacing and sat down next to Grace.

"It's not that I don't care. I think my priorities have shifted, that's all." Grace reached for his hand. "You're right. We don't need to do this. Maybe Dale did us a favor."

"What are you saying, Gracie?"

"I'm saying I don't know if I really know what love is, but maybe this is as close as I can get to it." She raised her eyes and met his. Love shone from his like she had never seen before. Her heart skipped a beat as she realized this was exactly what she had been waiting for.

"I love you." Xander waited.

Grace smiled. "I know you do. I see it in your actions every day, in your words when I read and reread the poem you wrote me. I don't know where to go from here, though."

"Maybe we just take one day at a time and figure it together as we go." Xander leaned forward and kissed her gently.

Chapter Thirty-Five

Xander and Grace talked for hours, finally deciding they would give up the inheritance, knowing that it would make neither of them happy. With a decision finally made, Xander felt a sense of relief and peace flowed over him. Grace finally was relaxed with him. She oozed relief at having decided to move on with *her* life, not what her mother wanted for her.

Xander groaned when his cell phone disturbed his peace. The last thing he wanted to do was interrupt this moment with Grace. He glanced at the caller ID: FATHER.

"Answer it." Grace stopped leaning against him and sat up.

"Hello, Father." Xander tried to keep the sarcasm out of his voice.

"Can you and Grace come over? We need to talk." There was no small talk, but straight to the point. So typically.

"About what?" Xander glanced at Grace.

"I heard about Dale being at your place. Please, Sebastian, come over."

"Fine. See you in a few." Xander clicked his phone off and looked at Grace. "We've been summoned to the Stevens' household for a talk."

Grace nodded. "You know it doesn't matter now. We know what we are doing."

Xander nodded, but couldn't ignore the pit in the bottom of stomach telling him something else was going to happen.

Just as they stepped onto the porch of the Stevens' homestead, Gerard swung open the door. "In the study, sir."

Xander nodded and with his arm around Grace approached the study. The door was half open and Xander paused before pushing it wide.

"Come in. Good to see you, Grace." John sat behind his massive desk. He seemed to have aged overnight.

Grace and Xander sat down in the chairs opposite John, and waited silently. John stood and came to the front of the desk, perching on the edge of it.

"Want to tell me what happened?" John looked at Xander.

"Not particularly. Sounds like you already know what happened?" Xander glanced at Grace. "We just want to know what your part of it was."

"I wasn't involved in this. I shut Dale off years ago, though I suspect your Mother still supports him thinking I don't know."

Xander nodded. "Where is she?"

"I heard you were here, dear." Elizabeth strode into the office, looking pointed down her nose at Grace. "Oh, and you brought company."

"No, I didn't bring company, Mother. Grace is family." Xander stood and kissed his mother on the cheek.

"Well, what brings you by and why are you holed up in this horrid room? John, you should know better than to bring them in here. The living room would have been more appropriate." Elizabeth gestured towards the door.

"We're in this *horrid* room because I thought it was the one place you wouldn't dare show your face."

Grace's eyes widened at the malicious in John's voice. This obviously was not a loving relationship. Xander reached for her hand and gave her a reassuring squeeze.

John stood and grabbed Elizabeth by the elbow, leading her around his desk and helping her into his chair. "But since you are here, why don't you tell us when Dale arrived back in town?"

"Dale's in town?" Elizabeth voice rose an octave.

"Well, we know he called you from jail and you told him he was on his own." Xander broke in, trying not to smirk at the shock on her face. "Just spill it Mother. We know more than you think we do."

"None of this would have happened if *she* had stayed away from you. Sebastian, you don't need to hobnob with the commoners."

Xander clenched his hands. "Commoners? Like you were Mother before you lied your way into a marriage with someone with money?"

Elizabeth rose. "You will not speak to your Mother that way, Sebastian."

"Sit down, Elizabeth." John took a step towards her. "I'm done. I'm done with your lies and always throwing money at you to make you happy when you have made my life miserable. It's over. You will pack your bags tonight. I will make a reservation for you in a hotel for tonight and tomorrow you will find yourself a place far away from here. I will give you a healthy divorce settlement, but it will stipulate that you will not come within thousands of miles of this town, myself, Xander or Grace. If you do, the money will stop and you will be on your own for good. Trust me, Elizabeth, this is nothing more than a pity settlement for you. I have no qualms with sending you away without a dime."

Xander watched his mother carefully. The tears pooling in her eyes were as fake as the fingernails she sported. With bravado that Xander had never seen before, John pulled Elizabeth's chair back. "I would start packing now, if I were you."

"You can't do this. I didn't do anything." Elizabeth pleaded with John.

"Except lie and cheat...be a snob...the list could go on." John gave her a little nudge. "Go pack."

"I will kill Dale. He's just like his father, useless." Elizabeth bit her lower lips as soon as the words left her mouth.

"It's not a secret, Mother. We all know that Father isn't Dale's biological father and that you lied to trick him into marrying you." Xander stated in a dry voice.

"I didn't trick John."

"Oh, please." John's voice rose with every word. Years of pent up frustration and anger came tumbling out of him. "You were jealous of Abigail from day one. We had had one date when you convinced yourself and your father that I was the one you were going to marry. My father went along with it only because your family came into some money just before the wedding. Had they not, he never would have entertained the idea."

Elizabeth took a step back and glanced between Xander and Grace. "It wasn't like that."

"It most certainly was and don't think for a second you can fool anyone else." John sank into his chair. "Get out, Elizabeth, now."

Xander watched his mother leave the room, shoulders slumped in defeat. "What now?" He turned towards his father.

"I don't know." John shook his head. "Grace, what can I do to make this right?"

Grace smiled. "Mr. Stevens, you didn't do anything to cause this. It's not your responsibility to make it right."

"You're very gracious, just like Abby." John nodded. "But I still feel I should be doing something."

Xander spoke up before Grace could answer. "We decided to walk away from the inheritance. Grace and I just want to live our own lives, not what Abigail thought she could manipulate for us."

John shook his head. "Don't give up on it. Abby wanted you to have that. I don't know why she did what she did for the stipulation, but please, let me help you get it back up and running."

"Insurance will pay for it and they will go after Dale to be reimbursed." Grace spoke. "It doesn't matter about Mom's reasons. Xander and I feel we would be better off following our own path."

"Together I hope." John watched Grace. "You are good for my son, Grace."

Grace's face flushed. "Yes, together. He's good for me." She glanced at Xander, and he felt his grin spread across his entire face.

Chapter Thirty-Six

Grace collapsed, exhausted. It had been a long day and the crux of it was the eye-opening division in Xander's family. John had shown a whole new side than Grace had him pegged for. Elizabeth, well she was the bitch that Grace had always known her as, however Xander seemed to be more relaxed around his father and that was a huge breakthrough in Xander's life of childhood hurt and insecurities.

Today had been a day of healing in so many ways. Grace had finally made a decision with Xander to move forward without working for the inheritance. It gave her a freedom from her own childhood insecurities and yet she didn't feel her mom would be disappointed at all. When they finally arrived back home, Grace had begged exhaustion and headed to bed. Although disappointment shined in Xander's eyes, he understood.

Grace lay in bed now with her mind whirling. As had become her habit, she pulled out the poem Xander had written. She had memorized it by now, but she carefully read the words again. There was nothing that could convince her anymore that Xander didn't truly love her. Every time she read the words, she had chills up her spine and tears in her eyes. She closed her eyes and savored the warmth that spread through her with the realization that she was loved.

She fell asleep with the poem pressed between her hand and her chest. Her dreams were filled with Elizabeth chasing after her, berating the fact that she was a commoner and not good enough for her son. Behind Elizabeth ran Dale, chasing his mother, begging for her forgiveness and for her love. Grace woke with a start, heart racing.

She reminded herself that it was just a dream and Elizabeth would be gone from their lives now that her and John were divorcing. She read the poem again, looking for relief of the anxiety that filled her. She wanted peace from the past and all that it held over her. Her own mother still reached from the grave, trying to control her life.

Grace pushed the covers back and glanced at the clock. Four a.m. She sighed. The night was over for her. She paced the floor and fought to control the anxiety that had plagued her for years whenever she thought she was letting her mom down. She shook her head to clear her mind. She knew deep down her anxiety was only in her mind, as her mom had never berated her when Grace did her own thing.

Resigned that sleep would elude her, she pulled a sweatshirt over her t-shirt and shorts. Coffee would wake her up and let her get back to the present. Her bare feet padded silently on the stairs, yet she had barely gotten to the bottom when she heard him.

"Can't sleep?" Xander's figure sat up front on the couch.

"Did you sleep down here?" Grace paused at the living room door.

"Not sure I'd call it sleep, but yes, I rested down here." Xander swung his feet to the floor and reached for the small lamp next on the end table. The dim light gave enough glow for Grace to see the lack of sleep evidenced in his face.

"I was going to make coffee." Grace pointed to the kitchen over her shoulder. "Want some?"

"Uh huh." Xander nodded.

Grace put on the coffee. While she waited for the brew, she opened a package of cinnamon rolls to pop in the oven to cook. Just as she finished prepping them, the coffee maker beeped, signaling as being done. She poured two mugs. Double checking that the timer was set on the oven, she grabbed the mugs and went to Xander.

She paused briefly as she studied him sitting on the couch, head tilted back with his eyes closed. His breathing indicated he was sleeping once again. She placed the mug on the coffee table and sat next to him. Sipping her own coffee, she watched him.

"Where's mine?" Xander smiled with his eyes closed. "I'm not that dead to the world that I can't feel you next to me."

Grace chuckled. "Right in front of you."

Silence filled the living room as Grace and Xander enjoyed their coffee, holding hands. Grace couldn't remember a time she felt so content in her life.

"You sure about the decision we made yesterday?" Xander's voice broke through her thoughts.

"Absolutely."

"We'll have to call Bob then and let him know. Is your apartment still available?"

Grace sighed. "I sublet it. So, no it's not."

Xander squeezed her hand. "We'll figure it out."

The timer on the oven rang and they spent the next couple of hours eating and drinking coffee while they shared their desires for their lives with each other.

The phone's ring startled them from their conversation. Grace glanced at the clock—just before eight. Who would be calling at this hour?

Xander reached for the phone. "Hello?"

"Xander. It's Bob. I have some interesting news for you regarding Abigail's will. Can I stop by?"

"Sure. Grace and I wanted to speak to you about that anyway." Xander mouthed "Bob" to Grace and she nodded.

"If you don't mind, I'd like to do this as soon as possible. Mind if I stop by this morning, in just a little bit?" Bob requested.

"Of course. We're up so anytime is fine." Xander hung up the phone and looked at Grace.

"Strange. Apparently interesting news regarding your mom's will."

"Hmmm. It doesn't really matter since we have decided to opt out of the inheritance." Grace got up and placed her mug and plate in the sink. "I'm going to shower before he gets here."

"We might as well hear him out. Who knows, maybe it will change your mind on opting out."

Grace shrugged. "I doubt it, but we'll see.

Chapter Thirty-Seven

Grace showered in record time, especially in light of the fact that she had gotten little sleep last night. Normally after a night with no sleep, she would linger in the shower, just letting the hot water run over her, taking her time waking up. After throwing on jeans and a T-shirt, Grace combed through her hair.

She stared at her reflection in the mirror. A wide eyed young woman stared back at her. Grace studied herself. She didn't look any different for being in love. Was something supposed to change with her? Love had always confused her. Was it because she had never truly experienced it before? She had never felt like she did when she was around Xander. She found herself missing him when he was gone and longing to see him again. She smiled. If this was love, she could live with it.

She skipped down the stairs to find Xander in the living room with Bob, having just arrived.

"Good morning, Bob." Grace slipped into the easy chair and folded her legs up under her.

"Good morning, Grace. Thank you both for seeing me on such short notice." Bob pulled out a folder from his briefcase. He glanced between Xander, sitting on the couch, and Grace in the chair. "I heard about the arrest of Dale for breaking and entering, and the arson. This is good news for the rebuilding of the barn."

Xander nodded. They both sat silently waiting for Bob to continue. Bob took a deep breath and exhaled slowly. "In light of new information, there has been a change in the will."

"What kind of change?" Grace sat forward.

"Grace, I need you to understand what I'm going to say is what I have observed and from you and I talking a bit the other day. I know you didn't want me to say anything, but my hands are bound by the will and my responsibilities to Abigail."

Grace shook her head. "I don't understand."

Bob handed each of them an envelope. "I was instructed to give these to you once it was obvious to me that you two were in love with each other."

Grace and Xander each took the envelopes. Meeting Xander's eyes, Grace managed a small smile. What did Mom do now?

"Go ahead and read them and then we can discuss the situation further." Bob sat back on the couch, waiting for Grace and Xander to open their letters.

Grace opened hers first. She closed her eyes as she pulled out the sheet of paper and unfolded it.

My dearest Grace,

You are my greatest treasure. I have seen you grown up to be a beautiful, intelligent woman. I'm sorry for what I can only imagine I have put you and Xander through. It was not my intent to cause you any heartache and if that has been the case, I am truly sorry. However, if you are reading this letter, you have found yourself in love with him. It is my wish that you find true happiness and I have always known in my heart that Xander would be perfect for you. My wish for you, Grace, is to open your heart and allow love to be received from him fully. Don't be afraid of this, as it is the greatest gift in life you can received.

All my love,
Mom

Grace looked up at Xander, tears spilling down her cheeks. After collecting her emotions and reining in the tears, she read the letter out loud to Bob and Xander.

Xander nodded as she came to the end of the letter. He opened his letter and pulled out the paper.

He cleared his throat and began reading it aloud so Grace and Bob could hear.

Xander,

I will begin by apologizing for the need to clip your wings for the moment. I knew when you originally found out about my insisting you stay for two years, you would have been furious. You are a free spirit, but I truly believe that has only been true because you never had a reason to stay put. My dear, if you are reading this letter, you have found your reason to never fly again, at least not solo. Be gentle with Grace. She fears change and that is partly my fault for never pushing her to fly away and do as she wanted. I trust you will give her the love she deserves and allow yourself to receive her love just as fully.

All my love,
Abigail

Xander stood, walking over to Grace to kneel in front of her. "You okay?"

Grace nodded. "She gave a gift even after her death that I never could have imagined…You."

"I love you, Gracie." Xander gave her a gentle kiss.

"And I love you." Grace laid her palm against Xander's cheek, running her thumb gently across his stubble.

Xander stood and turned to Bob. "So what does this mean for the inheritance?"

Bob smiled. "Well, Abigail was convinced that you two were going to fall in love. The stipulations on the inheritance are now lifted. She had an amendment put in that if at any time you fell in love, with each other of course, and it was obvious to others, the estate is yours free and clear. No need to run the therapeutic riding business."

Grace glanced between Xander and Bob. "Are you kidding me? She put us through all this just to see if we would fall in love?"

Bob nodded. "I knew you might be upset, Grace, but your mom's heart was in the right place, even if she didn't go about it the right way."

"Unbelievable."

"Grace. Does it matter? In the whole scheme of things, it is done. We were going to give up all this anyway and now it's yours."

"Mine? It's ours, Xander." Grace took a deep breath. "No, it doesn't really matter, but I can't help but be hurt by how manipulative Mom was being right up to her death."

Bob rose. "I'll leave you two to talk things out. There are a couple of papers you will need to sign and I will have those ready for you by tomorrow. Feel free to just stop in the office to sign." Bob hugged Grace. "If you have further questions, call me. Just think about it and let things sink in."

Grace nodded. She continued to sit there after Xander and Bob left the room. She could hear Xander talking softly to him before he left.

"Want to get out of here for a while?" Xander stood in the doorway.

Grace nodded. "Where to?"

"Lighthouse. Bring a sweatshirt. It will be cold this morning on the bike."

Xander turned and walked away. Grace sat there and reread her letter from her mom. She had been ready to give everything up for Xander and her mom had turned around and given her everything anyway…and then some.

Maybe it was time to just put the past behind them and move forward from here.

Chapter Thirty-Eight

Grace and Xander rode off with light hearts. Grace found herself relaxed, arms loosely around Xander's waist leaning against his back. She loved the feel of his muscles as he rode with the bike, his body moving as one with the motorcycle. She smiled in her helmet. This was the happiness that Mom had given her, in her own way. Abigail had given Grace not only permission, but a nudge in the right direction, to completely find both herself and love along the way.

There was nothing better than the feeling of freedom. They had no ties if they didn't want them. They could go off and do what they wanted. Grace had already taken a leave of absence from teaching. What was stopping them from just riding off and having an adventure?

When the motorcycle came to a stop at the lighthouse, Grace sat back. Xander waited while she got off the bike. She took off the helmet and placed in on the seat. She turned and walked to the rocky edge. She closed her eyes as the water sprayed off the rocks and the light spray hit her face. She kept her eyes closed as Xander came up behind her, wrapping his arms around her waist. She laid her head back against his chest and smiled. This was a life she could definitely get used to.

"What are you thinking?" He kissed her temple.

"That I want to ride off into the sunset with you and just explore new places." Grace opened her eyes, turning to look up at Xander.

"What about the house?"

"What about it? It isn't going anywhere and I already have a leave of absence from the school. Why not use it? Take me places, show me what you have already seen." She pleaded with him.

"We can go anywhere you want to, but there are still things we need to discuss about the house. The business." Xander entwined his fingers with her and pulled her to a large rock to sit down.

"We don't have to make any decisions right now. I'm not saying disappear forever." Grace stared at the waves hitting the rocks.

"Grace, I want to go with you. To show you things that you have been dying to see, I do, but suddenly I feel this huge responsibility that I can't just walk away from either."

Grace laughed sardonically. "Leave it to my mom."

"What?"

"She gives *me* freedom and *you* responsibility." Grace turned to Xander. "We'll figure it out, but I don't want to be stuck here forever."

"I don't want you stuck anywhere. I want you happy, always."

They sat in silence, both lost in their own thoughts of what their new lives would mean for them. Hours passed with hardly a word spoken between them before Grace stood up.

"Come on. Time to face reality."

They turned towards home, knowing the conversation was inevitable…a conversation that could leave one of them unhappy and the other miserable.

They arrived home to find John just getting out of his car. "Well, good timing I guess."

"What's up, Dad?" Xander took in the look of surprise at the term of Dad being used and realized it probably was the first time since he was kid that he had called his father that. Forgiveness apparently was in the works.

"Hi, John. Come on in." Grace looped her arm through John's and started up the stairs. "What brings you by?"

John waited until Xander had joined them before answering. "I, well…I meant what I said about wanting to mend fences. Xander, I'm so sorry for all those years of not being there for you."

Xander nodded. "It's okay. Let's just start fresh and move forward."

John smiled. "I would want nothing more."

"Good. How about staying for dinner?" Xander started towards the kitchen. "I'm going to marinate some steaks."

"Sounds good." John turned towards Grace. "There's something different about you two today."

Grace filled him in on the visit from Bob and how things now stood with the inheritance.

"Leave it to Abby to throw in a loophole."

"I can't help but feel that she was just playing games with our lives, but on the other hand, if she hadn't I probably never would have fallen in love with Xander, and that truly is a gift from her."

John nodded. "She always seemed to know what was best for everyone else. She had an intuitive nature that could sense things."

Grace and John joined Xander in the kitchen. "What does that mean for you and Grace now, with the business?"

"Not sure. Grace wants to do some traveling. Honestly, we haven't talked about it, but I was getting excited about marketing this new business and running it." Xander shrugged. "I guess I was looking forward to having a full time job right here."

"We can still do it, if you want."

"You want to go back to teaching. That is your true love, I know that." Xander shook his head.

"Well, now that Elizabeth is gone, I could use something that will keep me busy. Why don't I help out while Grace teaches?"

Xander looked at Grace. She nodded her agreement. "Fine. I guess we can discuss this over dinner, but for now, you might want to see what we have to do before committing."

Grace sat on the barstool watching father and son walk to the spot where the barn needed to be rebuilt. How appropriate, she thought. A rebuilding of Xander's relationship with his dad along with everything else. It was a time to move forward and she was so thrilled to have Xander beside her as they traversed this new adventure.

Together.

Acknowledgements

I would be remiss if I didn't acknowledge a few people who helped immensely with finalizing this book. Thank you to Dorothy Callahan, my beta reader/editor who gives amazing feedback. Thank you to Todd Aubertin for his never ending support in my writing career and his poetry that gave life to Xander's Poem. And last, but certainly not least, thank you to Sara Carbonneau, my editor, who believes in my writing and gently prods me to stick to my deadlines and helps me polish the final version.

Also Available from Emma Leigh Reed:

Mirrored Deception

Trusting Love

Second Chances

A Time To Heal

About the Author

Emma Leigh Reed lived in New Hampshire most of her life before moving to Tennessee. She has fond memories of the Maine coastline and incorporates the ocean into all her books. Her life has been touched and changed by her son's autism - she views life through a very different lens than before he was born. Growing up as an avid reader, it was only natural for Emma Leigh to turn to creating the stories for others to enjoy and has found herself an author of contemporary and romantic suspense. With a BA in Creative Writing/English, Emma Leigh enjoys sharing her knowledge with others and helping aspiring authors.

Made in the USA
Monee, IL
30 August 2021

76915902R00213